The Bus Shelter and Other Stories

D.S. Moran

Long Dash Publishing
368 Stratford Road
Brooklyn, NY 11218

www.longdash.com

ISBN -1-59899-192-2

For Eileen, not always right, but never wrong.

Acknowledgements

I wish to thank Barbara Katz Rothman, author of many books, for her editorial assistance and publishing savvy but most of all for her time, my teachers at Brooklyn College and the Prattsville NY Advocate for publishing many of my short stories. Kathy Donovan's timely help with the cover design is much appreciated.

Contents

Previously published stories are listed with citations at the back.

Beyond the Wicket Door

I drove my daughter and grandson to the mall last week and while she shopped I sat on a bench under a palm frond, under the central glass dome next to the wishing well pool and fountain, (re-circulated water, of course). Little Timmy, aged four, lounged against my knee and we licked our ice cream cones and watched the world walk by, one of my principal occupations since retiring eight years ago from the Fire Department. "Now don't let him wander off." My daughter probably said the same thing to Timmy. At first I only saw the back of the bald man ushering the eight year old into the Pay-Less Shoe Store, rather impatiently. I was hidden by the palms when he turned and glanced my way and he couldn't have seen me. Still, I sat up erect. Kevin was still as slim as ever after twenty years, even if the sparkle had transferred from his eyes to his bald head.

I had the early watch the morning Kevin and Walter, the two new Probies assigned to my company came crashing through the wicket door bringing a gust of January air with them. Their cheeks were rosy under spanking new serge caps with shiny silver badges. They had been laughing about something. They had to stoop a bit coming through the small door, which sat in the large apparatus door of the firehouse. Once inside they became a little subdued like in church. Their faces reacted to their smelling of the stale, old smoke that pervaded the old firehouse; it came from the long coat rack of fire coats with helmets sitting above and pairs of boots lined up below with owners' names and badge numbers printed on the turned down inside of the boots. Smoke residue seeped from the lengths of the 2 ½ inch cotton hose drip drying on the angled hose racks mounted against the far wall, the engine's hose bed and folded hose; and from the coal furnace bouncing on its foundation below in the cellar. I had ten years on the job, still had hopes of improving myself, of reforming the job. There were four regular chauffeurs and me, the relief or 'fifth wheel' who drove when one of the others was on vacation. Nylon hose, which didn't have to be dried out as cotton did to prevent rot, was just coming onto the job. The new masks were kept in suitcases; the wearing of, like cleaning of toilet bowls, was relegated to the Probies and junior men. The old timers were contemptuous of masks; they limited vision, gave a false sense of security, the helmet kept falling off, their bulk restricted movement.

Kevin and Walter were tall, young, eager and happy. They carried their stiff, new fire coats with clean, bright yellow horizontal lines over one arm, clutching their shiny new helmets in one hand and their new boots in the other.

"Dump your gear over here out of the way." I smiled, rising from the old swivel chair. "'Case, they have a run. Sign in, in the journal. In red ink. Only the Housewatchman writes in black."

"Wow. You still use the straight pens and ink wells?!"

"What do you mean, 'Wow'. We just got these. Last week we were still using quills."

"I heard this house had the horses."

"See the kitchen in the back? Used to be the stable. Go upstairs and see the lieutenant. He'll give you your group assignments. Then come down. We'll have coffee. Meet the other guys."

"Right. Hey, what did they do before the bells came in?"

2

"Drums."

Walter was twenty-seven, married with two small boys and lived about a dozen blocks from the firehouse. Kevin was twenty-two, single, played a lot of softball, lived at home. They were assigned groups opposite each other; the Captain kept Kevin, the senior Lieutenant took Walter. I could tell you what the officer was telling them upstairs. 'Rule number one: Don't be late. Rule number two: If you're going to be late, telephone. Rule number three: Don't be late. When we're at a fire, stay either with the officer or the M.P.O. (motor pump operator), AKA the chauffer. Walter, you come in tomorrow night. Kevin, you come in the following morning. What else? The guys will give you an empty locker. Find an empty spot on the rack downstairs and stow your gear. On payday or there about, you pay Commissary and House Tax. The guys will tell you about the routine. What else? Oh, welcome aboard.'

Walter and Kevin fell into the firehouse routine; they washed toilet bowls, dishes, the apparatus floor, the fire engine, polished the brass poles that we slid down during the night to save time. Four months went by, and now with six months on the job they exchanged their orange probie helmet front pieces for the black ones we all wear in the engines, with our company numbers and badge numbers. In the 'trucks', Hook and Ladders, they wear red front pieces. We are color-coded. Walter and Kevin went to their first car fires, trash fires, operating the booster line off the back of the rig. "Don't stick your face in that barrel! There might be a bottle or an aerosol can ready to go off like a grenade. Stick the line in the barrel, not your face. Got it?" "Got it"! They went to their first mattress fire; stretching the line to the third floor, down the smoke filled hall, through the railroad flat apartment to the rear bedroom, (It was always the rear bedroom.), drenching the walls until the officer directed the nozzle towards the mattress. They got a belly full of smoke, they were directed towards the window, they found out how sugar sweet the outside air can be. They retched, black rubber bands of snot flowing from their nostrils, eyes stinging, lungs burning, legs wobbly, throat raw, head pounding. They knelt limp against the smashed window frame, head lolling, eyes beginning to focus on the people below in the street; the cop on the opposite sidewalk, hands in pockets, clean and dry, looking up at the smoke boiling from the fire apartment windows. 'Kee=rist! Why didn't I take that cops test?' Walter and Kevin, and their turn-out gear no longer smelt like an Army and Navy store; they smelt like the rest of us; smoke, grime, sweat, melted plastic, dog shit, wet plaster, garbage.

Two years went by. They grew in wisdom, cockiness, and humility and back to wisdom. Not many of us socialized together off the job but we had our promotion parties, twenty-year parties, Saint Patrick's Day Parade, retirement parties, the company picnic and the Christmas party. These were where the biggest fires were fought. And each year they grew bigger with the telling.

Walter would bring his sons around to the firehouse. The oldest, Walter Jr., about seven or eight was bug eyed, climbing all over the rig, sitting behind the wheel, jumping up and down on the back step. The younger one, Charley, maybe six was rather timid and hung by his father or mother by the front door, shaking his head at the urgings of little Walter who, when he called Charley a baby, caught a crack across the head by Walter, Sr. Sometimes Walter's wife, Marion was with them and someone

4

would shout, "Matron in Quarters." the password to watch your language. Little Walter looked just like his father, blond, Nordic-like. Charley favored his mother, dark hair and brown eyes. Marion was quiet but you could see she was proud as punch of the three of them. It was Kevin who got Charley over his shyness about the smelly, dark firehouse and showed him over the whole place, from the coal pile in the cellar to the bunkroom and the offices. Charley always looked for Kevin, who would usually be working when they visited.

One Friday night just before the Fourth of July weekend Kevin was going off a day tour and Walter was coming on his last night before a short vacation. He had rented a bungalow out on Long Island for two weeks near the beach. Kevin would relieve Walter in the morning, officially at 0900 hours, but you could leave early if someone came in and rode for you.

Walter carried his gym bag of clean clothes Marion sent him to work with once a week. "Hey, Kev, can you come in early in the morning? I want to make a fast break out of the city if I can, beat some of the beach traffic."

"Sure, Eight"?

"Great, bro. Got this new, or almost new surfcasting rod I'm dying to try out. Marion and the kids will pick me up here and we're gone. I just packed the station wagon. We have to bring all our own linen and towels. Can you believe it, for what they're charging?"

"You're getting out at the right time. The TV five-day forecast says in the nineties for the next week."

"You playing ball tonight?"

"Yeah, Marine Park."

"Who?"

"105, 219."

"Piece of cake."

"We wish. See you."

"See you."

I was the covering chauffer that night. The night was quiet, a car fire, third due on an 'All Hands'. The company didn't even stretch. Three false alarms. At eight a.m. Walter was standing in the doorway, straining at the bit, looking for Marion and the station wagon, and Kevin to appear. The rest of the crew were having coffee in the kitchen. A box came in to which we responded on the Second Alarm. At 8:14 it went to an All Hands. You could hear the chairs scrape back away from the kitchen table. Sitting at the Housewatch desk, I said, "Walter, did you gas the rig after that last run?"

"Done."

It was just a little too early for anyone to be in to relieve Walter, who walked out onto the apron, craning his neck, willing Kevin to show up. Kevin was known to go out with the boys after a game. Maybe he got lucky and didn't even go home. Joe, my relief strolled into quarters with the News under his arm.

"What?"

"An All Hands over on Ocean. We go on the Second."

At 8:20 the fire went to a Second Alarm. Joe jumped up on the box and kicked over the rig, the lieutenant slid the pole, Walter ran back inside and jumped into his boots; "Shit!" everybody jumped on the rig and they were away, going around the corner on two wheels as Kevin came running around the same corner. He held up his hands, palms up in a gesture of apology to Walter who swung from a strap on the back step. Walter shrugged and smiled, and they were gone, racing down the avenue. Just then

6

Marion and the kids pull up with the station wagon, looking like the Grapes of Wrath. I said, "Kevin, get your gear, ride over to the fire with Marion and relieve Walter. And everybody will be happy."

"What is it?" said Marion

I said, "A supermarket over on Ocean Avenue."

Just then a, 'probably will hold with the present assignment' came over the department radio.

I said, "They got it knocked down. Walter will probably be waiting for you in the street. He can leave his gear on the rig. Kevin will take care of it. Hey, guys, have a nice time at the beach." They rode away with Charley sitting on Kevin's lap. Kevin was tickling him.

The supermarket was new, with a large truss roof; bowed rafters, rounded like an airplane hanger. The height between the ceiling and the roofing was as much as six feet. There was a lot of wiring and ducts in there. The store was evacuated and the trucks were still searching in the heavy smoke condition for the main body of fire. Lines were stretched into the interior and onto the roof. There were two truck companies and another engine besides ours on the roof. The trucks were making exploratory holes above where they suspected the fire to be hidden. There was nothing for the engine companies and their hose lines to do on the roof until some fire was exposed. It was a sunny day, little wind, the smoke rising lazily out of the chocked open doorways. Kevin got Marion, Walter and Charley through the fire lines and left them across the street from the fire building while he crossed and made his way up a ladder to relieve Walter. Walter came to the edge of the roof and the boys saw him and jumped up and down, cheering. Marion shaded her eyes to see him and waved nervously. Walter waved back and someone

7

behind him called to him. He turned away from the edge of the building and out of view. Just as Kevin reached the top of the ladder the roof exploded and collapsed. Fifteen or sixteen men fell into the opening. Some fell directly onto shelves of canned goods; others were caught in the wires holding up the suspended ceiling. The main body of fire had been boiling away in the large cockloft within the wooden trusses. Walter and five other men were caught like spiders in the web of heat and air conditioning ducts, and the miles of wiring that crisscrossed the space above where the ceiling had been. Men rushed in from the street, fighting their way through the maze of canned goods, overturned shelves of cleaning products, dog food, bread, etc. The men who they could reach with hooks, they pulled down from the spider web, victim and rescuer alike splashed with the molten tar from the roof and falling burning debris. They could not reach Walter and five others with their standard six-foot hooks. Ten and fifteen footers were called for. No one could reach them from the roof. No one could later say they heard any of them cry out. Maybe ten minutes passed before they could get to them with portable ladders from within the store. Alarm bells on Scott Masks were going off all over the store but no one left the building. As masks went empty, face pieces were ripped off and fresh air was done without.

Across the street, Marion Walter and Charley flattened themselves against a store window, frozen in apprehension. Waiting and waiting for Walter to reappear at the edge of the roof.

A Third and Fourth Alarm were transmitted. But even before they arrived, with the fire exposed it was rather quickly knocked down, slowed only by the rescue operations.

The Fire Commissioner responded, the Department Chaplains responded, EMT's responded. Pieces of paper flew across news desks, firemen in fire houses all across the city were glued to the department radios or paced the apparatus floors like caged panthers, wives and mothers of firemen clutched their throats as they were told, 'Big fire in Brooklyn, a lot injured. Roof collapsed. Maybe some dead." "Is Steve working today?"

Kevin stood frozen to the top of the ladder for what seemed like a long time. Then he hopped onto the roof and moved closer to the center of the collapsing roof until someone took him around the waist and dragged him back to the parapet of the building. When he undressed that night there were red welts on his chest and stomach where the heat had been conducted through the rivets of the metal clasps of his turnout coat. Black and purple bunting was hung across the fronts of three firehouses. Four days later there were six Fire Department Line of Duty funerals, Walter's in Brooklyn, two in Queens, one in Nassau and two in Suffolk. They were all married, fourteen children were fatherless. Almost everyone off duty attended, some to two or more funerals. Many of the members in the long, not so straight rows of blue serge uniforms standing at attention in the streets in front of the churches where the funeral masses were said had bandaged ears, necks, and hands

It took a long time and a lot of cajoling for us to shake Kevin out of his depression, even a little. He could not face Marion or the boys. She came up to him at the wake and hugged him for a long time. When she released him he had to leave the funeral parlor. Time and again he announced he was resigning. Fireman after fireman related similar stories to him of how they had undergone the same situations. Give it time. "Be the best fireman you can be. That's the best thing you can do for Walter." I had been the last one to see and speak to both of them on that last night. After a while Kevin transferred to a truck in another battalion. They needed him at first base. Whenever we got together, no matter what we talked about it always ended on that day on the apron in front of the firehouse, on the rig turning the corner, on the ladder, with Marion and the boys waving from across the street. It became like trying to change the subject from aviation while plunging through the clouds in a 747 at four hundred miles an hour. As the years went by, Kevin and I, I tell myself, unconsciously avoided each other at department affairs, increasingly reluctant to view again that fateful filmstrip. We would wave across the room enthusiastically at each other at affairs but neither made a big move to cross the room. Maybe I was the only one to hear Kevin say he would be in early on that last morning? After all, I was relieved. I could have ridden for Walter. But that just wasn't done. Chauffeur for chauffeur and Probie for Probie. That's the way it's done. The best thing I could do for him was to get lost. That's why I sit now hidden behind my palm frond, my grandson's ice cream cone dripping on my khakis.

THE BUS SHELTER

"This is Fiction 101." I droned for the fourth year. We met on Tuesdays and Thursdays from seven to nine. There were twenty students in the evening class. "Do we have any English majors here?" Three raised their hands. The rest I knew were business and science. I know most of these people work all day and are just filling their core curriculum, so many credits Humanities, etc. During the summer I racked my brain for a way to light a fire under them, get them interested in literature, without using the word 'literature', how they could get a better handle on the big picture rather than through history or biology. One lug in the back was already dozing. Some were doodling in their spiral notebooks. The English majors jotted some notes. I closed the classroom door as the hall quieted down.

"Tonight's going to be easy. I'm going to tell you a short story. Take notes or not as you wish. You're not kids anymore. Just one thing. No questions. We'll call it "The Bus Shelter".

Alice Klepper slowed the Saab and stopped at the red light. It was a long light. Next to her was a bus stop. One elderly gentleman in a gray suit with a cane waited under the bus shelter. He had been taller but was now bent with the years. His receding white hair curled over his shirt collar. She enclined her head to look at him and he turned towards her. He smiled, his eyes crinkling. He made an almost imperceptible bow in her direction. Her heart raced.

The driver of the car behind her began honking. Alice pulled over to the curb and caught her breath. When it was safe she got out and walked slowly back towards the bus shelter. The man was looking for the bus. She touched his sleeve shyly. He turned, smiling. We can not hear what they are saying with the roar of the traffic. She seems to shift her weight from one foot to the other like a nervous high school girl. She speaks rapidly, gesturing, pointing at him, at herself, head bobbing from side to side. He smiles but looks around slyly, uncomfortably. As she continues, a look of recognition enters his face. He looks up at the sky and heaves a great sigh. Now he looks at Alice as someone he has known a long time. She points to her car. He looks back towards the bus, then at the ground, then at Alice. He says something. She flings her arms around him, burying her cheek in his chest. He pats her elbow. She leads him to the car and opens the passenger door for him. He bows and gets in. She scurries around, gets in and drives off.

Alice Klepper did not come home that night to her wonderful husband Jim of thirteen years and her three beautiful boys, Sean, Richard and Brian. The schools called Jim's office and he had to pick the boys up and bring them home.

Alice and Roy as his named turned out to be drove north on the Interstate until Roy pointed out a certain exit. They drove along a state road and then a gravel road to a large cabin on a lake. They walked down to a dock and watched the sun set. Inside, Roy made a cozy fire in the stone fireplace. Alice and Roy sipped wine, curled up on the plaid couch. They hardly spoke. Later, she made tuna fish sandwiches and cocoa. The bedroom was unheated, for a short while.

"Where's mom? "Where is mommy?" "What about supper?" "Mommy is shopping."

"Are you going to make dinner, dad?"

"No. How about pizza?"

"Yea, pizza!"

As the little savages devoured the pizza, Jim roamed the living room, calling all her friends from his cell phone trying to sound casual. On some he left messages. But you can't fool women. All the while keeping an eye on the phone on the end table. He thought about calling the hospitals. He wanted to make himself a drink in the worst way.

Richard said, "Dad, are you going to eat yours?"

Jim looked at the two limp slices, "No. You guys split it." Brian pushed a half-eaten slice around his plate, saying "Choo choo, choo choo."

Sean went over and turned on the TV.

Jim said, "Turn that off. Get upstairs and do some homework." Sean and Richard knew he meant them. They looked at each other; well at least we tried, maybe later. They trooped up the stairs. "I'll be up to check. I better see action." To be able to exercise some control kept Jim off the ceiling, for now.

Brian drifted over; his mouth a splotch of tomato sauce, and wrapped his arms around Jim's leg and began to whimper. Jim bent and tousled his hair, "Where's Teddy? Find Teddy, Brian."

At any other time it would be funny, dragging Brian back and forth across the living room like a ball and chain. He thought where is that selfish bitch? Call in, at least. How many cold meals had Alice hung over where he hadn't called in? He couldn't really recall her ever falling off the radar. He put the phone in his shirt pocket and hoisted Brian. He took him into the kitchen and wiped off his mouth and then wiped his face. "Mommy will be home soon. If mommy sees you crying, mommy will start crying. You don't want to make mommy cry, right?" Brian hiccuped and sniffled. Jim held a tissue to his button nose, "Blow. Blow like the wind." Brian blew as hard as he could.

13

Jim had a thought and jogging Brian up and down, began looking around the kitchen for a note, a post-it, something that said Alice had said she would be late, the refrigerator door, a find for an archeologist of the twenty-fifth century, all the notes, dentist's and pediatrician's cards, dry cleaners, PTA schedules, soccer schedules, the calendar, the phone pad, the always missing pencil. He picked up the phone to make sure it was working and hung up. He was somehow comforted by the mess the boys had left, normalcy, the pizza box, the crusts, the unfinished soda glasses. You could tell the mother wasn't home, soda instead of milk. "But, dad, you always have to have soda with pizza."

He resolved to start on the hospitals if she hadn't checked in by the time he had Brian in bed. Jim trudged up the stairs, undressed Brian and made him sit on his potty on the commode with Teddy. He checked on Sean and Richard. Sean was reading a history book; Richard had a workbook open before him.

Sean said, "So, anything?"

"No. This will all turn out to be my fault. Mom probably told me something this morning that went in one ear and out the other. Show some progress, you two. I'll take heat for the pizza as it is."

Sean said, "Thanks for the pizza, dad."

Jim's throat tightened. He couldn't remember Sean ever thanking his parents for anything. He looked at Richard, always silent. What was he thinking?

The phone rang. They all started. Jim raised a finger and darted into his bedroom.

"Hello, Mary. Thanks for getting back to me. No. Nothing. Yeah, I tried her. I may try the hospitals." He listened for awhile shifting from one foot to

14

another. "Listen, Mary, I'm trying to keep this line open, you know? Yes, I appreciate that. I have to hang up now. Goodbye."

Bitch, he thought. She knows nothing. Just trying to pump me for gossip. There would be two other calls like that. The other few men and mostly women he spoke to knew enough to be brief.

Sean and Richard with the ears of dogs could put it together just from the tone of dad's voice. Richard just stared at his workbook. Sean whispered, "Look. Dad's always screwing up, right? And mom never does, right? She'll be home any minute, I bet you."

Jim looked in on Brian and Teddy, sleeping, for now. He tiptoed downstairs and took up the phone book. Hospitals. He called six, nothing. He sat staring at the blackness beyond the living room window. He got up and put on more lamps. He thought he heard car wheels crunch in the driveway and rushed to the window. It was a couple of doors down.

Jim went into the kitchen, put some ice in a tall glass and filled it with flat soda from the two liter bottle on the table. God forbid they should ever put the cap back on. But he couldn't get annoyed with them.

Jim settled into his chair in the living room, set the glass on the rug and fell instantly into a stupor. Just as quickly he awoke three hours later and stared at the blank TV screen. Alice. The boys. School. It was so quiet. He heaved himself up and went upstairs. Brian and Teddy were out. He covered them. Sean and Richard were asleep but with their clothes on. It was like camping. Mom would never have allowed that. He pulled their covers up.

Jim sloshed cold water in his face, dried off and drifted into the bedroom. The bed was made. It made him think of a hotel. The room said Alice. Smelled Alice. He opened a dresser drawer, the magic sock drawer. He thought I could shake her till her head fell off. Oh, God help us. Maybe she was kidnapped? We have no money. Maybe she was attacked. Knife point. Lying in a ditch, cold, alone, her panties shredded and bloody. He put his head down on his forearm and heaved a great sigh. God, got to stop this.

Nobody has called all night. No news is good news, right? He looked at the bedside clock, 6:10 a.m. The kids have to get up for school, lunches, homework, have to make some calls. He looked out the window. It was morning. The sky was blue. Only his car sat in the driveway. All so quiet. Then he realized, it was Saturday. Thank God. The boys were still quiet. They were exhausted, too. Well, let sleeping dogs lie. Where was that bitch! He could strangle her. God, don't do this to us. For the boys. Never mind me.

Brian was howling. The day had begun. Jim trooped into his room. He retrieved Brian and Teddy. Brian was wet. What else is new? "Get up, you two!" He got them all changed and cleaned up. "Where's mom?" "Is mom home?" "Where is mommy?" "Why isn't she here?" "Shut up! Don't you think I'd tell you if I knew? I want to know where mommy is too. She's probably visiting and forgot to tell us."

Jim had them around the kitchen table with orange juice.

Sean said, "Maybe Aunt Lois knows where mom is. Did you call Aunt Lois?" Sean and Richard looked accusingly.

Lois, that crazy bitch. He could never believe they were really sisters. Lois lived three hundred miles away. Thank God for small favors. She was a

16

blackjack dealer, floating from casino to casino. Three years ago, they had Brian in intensive care for a week with an unknown illness. Alice wouldn't leave his side. They set up a cot for her. After his temperature stabilized, they kept him there for another week. They never found out what the matter was. Sean and Richard were in preschool. They cried all the time. Jim and Alice had no parents. The closest relative was Lois.

After the first week, Jim was run to his knees. Lois roared into the driveway in a 1942 Packard convertible with an obscene air horn, 'Boom boom, let's go back to my room.' The boys loved her. She was something different. She put the house in order. She made Jim shower and change and sleep. He brought fresh clothes to the hospital for Alice. Lois made him pick up flowers for Alice. She sent Jim back to his office and took the boys to the track, the clubhouse at the trotters. They were underage but Lois knew people everywhere. The boys had BLT's and shakes. The day was half over. She gave them each six dollars. "Now pick a horse, preferably one with four legs, in the 6th, 7th and 8th races. Pick a name that appeals to you. I'll place the bets for you. If you win, great. If you lose, no crying. Get it? If you lose you gotta be a mensch. That's how you play the big game."

"What's the big game?" asked Sean.

Lois, in sunglasses and floppy hat, lowered her small, pearl binoculars, "The big game is life, Sean. Where everybody crosses the finish line and there are no scratches and no do-overs."

A big shot sitting quite near was smoking a large cheap cigar. The smoke was drifting towards the boys. Richard coughed.

"Say, sweety, could you take that smokestack over a few tables? I have children here."

He shrugged, "They shouldn't even be in here."

Lois lowered her glasses and bent towards him, staring, her face turned to stone.

The man next to him said something and they moved to another table.

When they got home, Jim was scandalized. The track!

When the boys were in at the TV, Lois said, "Lighten up, will you. It was like going to the park and the zoo all rolled into one." She had cautioned Sean and Richard about telling dad about betting. Sean won on the last race after Lois guided his pencil. Richard won the 6th, 7th and 8th. The kid was a natural. "Dad will confiscate the dough if you blab."

Jim reasoned it can't hurt to call Lois before he called the police. If she wasn't in, he'd leave a message.

He looked at the boys, "All right, all right. I'm calling." It rang twice. He hoped she wouldn't answer so he didn't have to talk to her.

Lois lay on her back with a big sleep mask. She groped for the phone, "What the fu.", pressing it to her ear. When she heard "Jim Klepper", she sprang into a sitting position and whipped off the mask, "What is it? Who's sick? An accident? What?"

Jim told her all he knew from picking up the boys from school. "I'm going to call the police now." The boys were watching him. He held up a finger and drifted into the living room. "Listen, Lois, if you know anything, tell me. I don't care what it is. The boys are right here, yeah."

Lois took a deep breath, "I always thought I knew Alice pretty well. If there were another guy, she never let on to me. We'll get to the bottom of this.

Let me make a few calls. I'll be over there in about four hours."

"No, Lois I don't want..."

"Yeah. I can just see that kitchen sink now." Click!

Jim looked at the sink. It was full.

"Listen I have to make one call and then we'll have pancakes."

"Yeah. Dad, I didn't know you could cook."

"Just keep it to yourselves. Sean, take down the Aunt Jemima and two eggs. Milk, syrup, plates, you know?

Jim sat on the couch and called the police. A detective, Stan Mahovac took down all the particulars of Alice and her car. He asked questions Jim would never have thought of, like what were her hobbies. He would be over in an hour or so. He would need a photograph of Alice. He would like to talk to Jim out of the boys' presence. If his wife made contact in the meantime, call him. "Sometimes people have to get off by themselves and let off a little steam. Hang in there."

While devouring the pancakes, Jim asked what they liked about Aunt Lois.

Sean piped right up; "She's cool. She takes us places. She's not always on our case."

Jim said, "You know what the difference between parents and aunts are? Parents are responsible every day, night and day. Aunts and uncles drop in and drop out. Especially when it gets hot. What about you, Richard?"

Richard shrugged, "Aunt Lois smells nice."

Brian said, "When is mommy coming home?"

When Detective Mahovac came in, Jim sent the boys out to the yard with the basketball.

"Mr. Klepper, what do you do?"

"I'm an attorney with Lane Thomas in the Centennial Building."

"Good. Then you understand the value of truth. Now I may ask some painful questions. But don't worry. Most of this will remain between you and me. If you lie or withhold, you might send us off in the wrong direction."

Jim clutched his hands and nodded.

Now, first of all, this happens every day. Usually it's the husband who runs away to the South Seas with his paint set. One woman and four guys. Do you guys put the toilet seat down after peeing?"

"Not always. I always tell her, a dry seat up is better than a wet seat down."

"I have three daughters, three cells, two regular phones plus the junk in my car. I give orders; I make rules, curfews, nothing. They get even".

"How?"

"They use my razor, replace the numbers on my cell with their girlfriends", whatever.

"Now, did your wife ever show any interest in learning to tap dance, play the violin or write the great American novel? Anything like that?"

"She is a great reader."

"Like what?"

"Short stories mostly."

"Romance, westerns, crime, sci-fi, international intrigue, what"?

Jim pointed to a bookshelf, "Easier if you look for yourself."

"Right. I'll check them out. Do you have the photograph? Good." The detective scrutinized the picture.

He scribbled in his notebook. "Now, can you think of anyone else I should speak to? Get a different slant."

"She doesn't work. PTA, soccer, three boys keep her busy enough. She has a sister who'll be here later."

"Good. Ask her to call me." He handed Jim his card and stood up. "I guess that'll be it for now." At the door he asked, "Oh, by the way, are you carrying on an affair with anyone?"

"What? No. No."

"We'll be in touch. Oh, and if you should receive a ransom note, call me, but not on the house phone."

Jim was out shooting baskets with the boys when he heard the obscene claxon of Lois's car a block away. Sean at twelve was making Jim sweat for his points. He was glad of an excuse to stop.

Lois took charge. Brian clung to her, accepting her as a surrogate. Sean alternated between missing his mother and wondering where Lois would take them.

On Monday Alice's disappearance was on page one below the fold. On Wednesday a small follow up on page eight.

Jim and Lois got the boys back in school and kept them busy after school. Lois stayed two weeks and engaged a competent housekeeper to take over. Slowly, some sort of routine around food, shelter and bathing set in for the Kleppers. Jim lost a few pounds. The incoming calls dwindled to nothing. His doctor gave him a prescription for 5 mg. Ambien. One woman at work tried to take him out for drinks. Detective Stan said we'll call you if anything develops, (It's not all about you.). At one point Jim sat Sean and Richard down and said, "Listen, one of the sad facts of life is that there will always be more questions than answers."

When Alice was thirteen and had been having her period for four months, she stood at the bus stop and took stock of herself. She knew her life was changing. She smelled differently. Her saliva tasted different. One minute she felt mature and sexy, and the next she couldn't stand her body. She would sometimes stutter. Boys she had never noticed caught her attention. She kept checking her breasts for growth. Girls she had admired and envied now looked silly the way they threw themselves at boys Alice thought were real jerks.

A powder blue convertible stopped for the light. The driver threw his right arm across the creamy leather seat-back. He squinted up at the red light. He turned towards Alice and smiled, Hi. Nice day. He had wavy dirty blond hair; a dark tan set off his white teeth. Her attempt at a smile came off as a rictus grin. Her effort to stand tall turned her back into a drawn bow. One hand clutched her stomach. She told her bladder, don't you dare. Her other hand pressed a hanky to her mouth. She stepped back and plopped on the bench. She could not take her eyes off him. He was gorgeous. He looked up at the light again and back at her. Some concern in his face. He smiled again. The light changed and he was gone but not gone. Alice put her head down almost between her knees and waited. When she slowly sat up, her breathing returning to normal, the world was changed. Colors were more vivid. People were more distinctive. Everywhere she looked was a picture waiting to be drawn. She had reprioritized her life. She was in love. That night she told herself it would all probably fade away in a day or two but it never did, never.

Three months after moving in with Roy, Alice woke up at dawn and felt his cold hand. His face was like marble. She tucked the blanket up around his chin and got up and made coffee. He had left a letter for

Alice. Alice waited until 9 o'clock and called his sister. They had never spoken before but the sister knew what it was all about. She would make all the funeral arrangements. There was no need for Alice to stick around. Roy had left Alice money. She got a motel room and from the obituaries learned of the place and time of the funeral. She sat in a shadowy corner and hardly heard all that went on.

The next day she called home. A woman answered. She called Jim's office. He said come home. He would meet her there. When Jim rushed in the door, he said, "Where the hell have you been?"

Alice shrugged, "It was some sort of amnesia. I don't know."

Jim said, "Should I get the boys out of school?"

"No. Let them finish the day."

"Amnesia, eh?"

"Not really, but let's tell the boys that for now."

"I don't know what to say. Our lives are changed forever."

"If you want, I'm home. If not I'll leave before the boys get home."

"No. I'm glad you're home for the boys. For myself I don't know. We'll tell them amnesia. That's good. When they get off the bus I'll go out and speak to them first. Break it gently, so to speak."

"They finally got the bus system going."

"They passed the bond issue."

Alice had tears in her eyes. She reached out a hand to Jim.

He stood still, "It's not the time, the three months, it's the not knowing. Not knowing every morning. Not knowing every night where you were. In court, in the supermarket. Whether you were ..."

When the boys came in, Sean said, "Hello." His voice was changing. He was growing out of his

23

clothes.   Brian clung to his father's trouser leg, "Where's Aunt Lois?"   Richard hung his head awkwardly.

The bell rang in the hall.   I glanced around the classroom. They were all attentive.

Someone said, "Well, what happened?"

"I said 'No questions.'"

I started to put on my coat. "Here's your homework for Tuesday.   Finish the story (moans and groans). You have five nights to work on it and five days to think about it. I want a first draft on Tuesday. Typed of course.

"What if we can't remember it all?"

"I'll bet you can give me a rundown on every game of the last World Series.   If you can't remember something, I guess it wasn't too important. Have a nice weekend." I whirled out the door.

ST. ALBAN'S COUNTRY CLUB

St. Alban's Naval Hospital had been built on the site of an old beautiful golf course. From an administration building radiated wooden corridors with walls filled with windows and French doors leading to colorful flower beds and broad green lawns. While on leave from Korea I became ill each night with chills and fever, and turned myself in to the hospital with malaria. Filled with vivacious young men with relatively minor wounds the hospital was cheerful. In my ward were several very elderly men who I learned were retired sailors entitled to stay there by some ancient law predating the VA. They dosed me with Permaquin and had me on fire watch duty in the deserted weekend corridors. One torrid Sunday a nurse wheeled an elderly man to a window so he could sit in the sun. He made me think of the newspaper photos of Spanish-American War Veterans leading the Memorial Day Parade from an open touring car. After a while the sun moved, leaving him in shadow. I asked if he would like to be moved into the sun. He nodded assent. The summer heat was beginning to get to me but he reveled in it in his cotton p.j's and robe. "Boy, it's hot, eh?" I said. His greatest movement was his head tremor. He said, "Stuck in Bombay three weeks in the heat." To show how salty I was, I said, "What happened, run out of coal?" His brow registering impatience, he said, "No wind!"

While You Were Out, Frankie Called

"Hello? Hello. Frankie? Frankie, where the hell are you? Your mother's worrying sick. You don't write. Not even a card. You can't make a phone call? What a time to call. You just missed your mother. It's 8:30 here. This is Wednesday. You know she goes to Bingo every Wednesday night. What's the matter with you? You just missed her. What? Oh, you didn't want to talk to her. Listen, Frankie. Regardless of everything, she's still your mother. Yes, yes. But if I can forgive, you can forgive. Don't be so righteous. Don't be so quick to judge. It's none of your business, anyway. What happened was between me and your mother. It's nobody's business but hers and mine.

You're damn right. No, I'm not getting pumped up. I don't get pumped up anymore. I've learned to cope. I vent.

Cosmo who? A magazine. You know I don't read magazines. If it ain't in the <u>News</u> I don't read about it. Just don't judge your mother. I'm no saint.

No, I never cheated on your mother. Not that it's any of your business. But I can understand. I'm not the easiest guy to live with. Yeah, don't tell you. You're a chip off the old block. I can tell you that. That time with the hip. When I had to get the hip replaced. I was drinking a lot. I couldn't work. I couldn't climb the ladder. Yes, I was depressed. It wasn't easy for her. You know how she likes to go out. To dance. And there's me with the cane schlepping along behind.

It happens.

No, I'm not a sucker. I'm just older and wiser. Maybe some day you'll grow up. There's more to

26

marriage than sex. Frankie, here's a tip. Don't put the people you love on pedestals. That way you don't have to see them fall off.

Yes, yes, the old philosopher. Go ahead, laugh. See? I don't get mad, anymore. No, I got rid of the cane six months ago. If you'd call you'd know.

No, not back to work yet.

No, I think my days on the scaffold are over. Yeah, the old man wants to put me in the office. Me, at a desk! I don't know. I'll give it a shot, I guess. You can't do roofs with a plastic hip. Good as new, my ass. Hey, I count my blessings. When it happened, they said maybe I'd never walk again.

How do I know? When you get a little older you learn to read faces. They don't have to always say something. So, this must be costing you something. Calling all the way from L.A.

The sun is still out? Amazing. It's been dark here for an hour. So, are you still writing those stories or did you get a real job?

With NBC, really?

A sit com. What's it called?

Oh, no name yet.

$1,200. a week! Stop it. Who'd pay you $1,200.a week to write that crap?

All right, all right. I'm sorry. It's not crap. Now who's getting touchy?

You moved! We figured. Your mother's letters all came back, 'Moved. No Forwarding.' Hey, I'm the one's got to listen to her crying at night. I'm not pulling your chain. You wanted long hair. Did I say anything? You wanted to go to art school. Did I say 'No'? Who's more liberal than me?

A new car. What?

A Bentley. Used, of course.

27

Appearances, I understand. Hey, hey. What about this pile of junk you left in the driveway? Weeds are growing up through that hole in the floorboards. It's the eyesore of the block. A classic my ass. A pile of junk. You don't want it? I'm going to have the junk man haul it away. All right?

Your sister? Don't ask. She's living with some married guy over in Jersey. I don't know. West New York. Yeah, West New York, New Jersey. She was always willful. Always. The nuns couldn't do a thing with her. I wash my hands. I wouldn't let her in the house. I'm off the case.

Yes.

Why? Because it's my house, that's why. When it's your house, you do what you want. I'm not taking it out on you. Yeah, she calls.

No, I don't talk to her. Your mother talks to her. Sends her money, too. Thinks I don't know. It's her money. She can do what she wants with it. So, you have to call when your mother's not home. What's up?

What? You're getting married? Who'd marry you, Mr. Self- centered?.

Yes, she must be crazy. She works at NBC. She better hold onto her job the way you go through them like Kleenex.

Oh sure, you're settled down now. What's her name?

Inez? What kind of a name is Inez? That's not Italian. Oh, Spanish.

I just said,'Oh'. Can't I say 'Oh'? Don't get so touchy. You're just like your mother.

You do too take after her. For twenty seven years I'm watching the both of you.

All right, twenty eight years.

No, I didn't forget when you were born. I remember it like it was yesterday. It was the coldest February on record. The snow. I had to dig the car out three times that night so it would be ready to take your mother to the hospital. Don't tell me about birthdays. So, what does her father do?

A carpenter, really? What a coincidence.

He owns his own business? That's good. He can give you a job when NBC gets wise to you. I'm only kidding. Hey, I just thought. You call when your mother is out to Bingo. Now I have to tell her you're getting married. Thanks a lot, pal. Now I have to listen to the ranting and raving. The hair pulling. The tears. Between you and your sister, Marie. Listen, Frankie. I'm not telling her. You have to call back when she's in. Don't put me in the middle, Frankie. I'll kill you.

She'll say we conspired. I'm not telling her.

What? You sent the airline tickets already.

When? Two weeks. You booked us a room. Hey, Frankie, you forget: I don't fly in planes. No sir, not me. Sure she can go by herself. Why not?

The train? Amtrack? I don't know.

The meals are included? Three days on the train. See the country.

Maybe. Sounds o.k. But no flying. That's out. Just so you know. Trade in the tickets. I got it. But Frankie, you got to do this for me. You got to call back tomorrow night when your mother is in and tell her yourself.

What do you mean, 'be a man'?! You be a man! Do the right thing. Frankie, I'm begging you..Don't laugh. O.k.? Tomorrow night between eight and nine. She'll be finished with the dishes. She'll be in a good mood. I'll put up the storm windows. That'll shut her up. She's been after me for a week.

No, I can manage the step ladder. Don't worry. Just you better call, that's all. Or you won't see me out there.

Yeah, you too. What you said.

All right. Frankie, I love you! Are you happy?

No, it wasn't so hard to say. Be good.

Yeah, good by."

PASTA E FAGIOLI

Tessy Petrucci was seventy-six. She came to this country in 1919 as a toddler and seldom left the six-block radius around her Brooklyn home. From Fasano's Bread Store to Marzano's Funeral Home, from De Martino's Pork Store to St. Stephen's Church, an area almost the same size as the village in Sicily where her people came from. Since she broke her hip on the ice three years ago she never left the house without her cane, and seldom without either her daughter Carmela or her grandson Anthony to accompany her. Her husband Vincent was dead fifteen years, a fight on the docks with some young punks. She never got the details. The Longshoremen's Union was very good with her medical bills. There was no insurance. She had had to move in with her daughter and her husband Tony Fornucci.

Carmella was a poor cook. They were all glad Tessy was there to make the gravies, the lasagna, the stuffed shells, and the tortellini. Tessy's son-in-law Tony, although he kept a butana over in New York and was seldom home, attended Sunday dinner religiously, the family centerpiece of the week, the day when everybody pretended everything was all right in the family.

Tony when he was young was a stallion who drank only from his own trough, but now he was a goat who ate rags from everybody's garbage. Now that he had no hair and few teeth he fancied himself a Don Juan in a god-awful wig. He looked like he scalped a camel. When he did stay home, he and Carmella fought; he drank too much Chianti and she threw china at him (not the anniversary set). He

31

slapped her around. Tessy's room was on the first floor in the back because of her hip. The walls were thin but she heard nothing.

Her grandson, Anthony was twenty-nine but to Tessy still a boy. He worked for his father but he wanted to be something different, a different life, but nobody knew what.

Tony got off the docks early and opened a bowling alley. Then he opened another and another. They all had bars in them and cards in a back room. This was all a front. What he really did was launder money for don Luca. Every Monday two paisanos in nice suits came to the house with two gym bags full of money from don Luca. Tony, Carmella, Anthony and sometimes Tessy would sit around the dining room table and count it quickly; then Tony would sign a receipt and give it to the men. They were polite to Carmella and Tessy. They smiled but not with their eyes. They would take nothing to drink. Over the next two days Tony and Anthony would distribute the money among the three bowling alleys and some stores with video arcades.

One night Tony came home drunk, waving a full-length mink coat in a plastic bag, not even in a box Tessy noticed. He made Carmella try it on. "Twirl around. Let me see what it looks like. It was dark on the back of that truck." He dribbled wine down his shirtfront. And people wonder why we leave the plastic covers on the furniture, mused Tessy.

"But Tony," giggled Carmella, "It's way too small for me. Look. I can't move my arms."

"So what? Who said it was for you. I just wanted to see what it looked like in the light. Take it off. And don't tear the lining. I'll smack you."

Carmella threw the soup tureen at him. He smacked her good against the wall, against the picture with the little light bulbs behind the windows in the Doge's Palace in Venice.

The next day Anthony had to take his mother to the dentist. She had two cracked teeth.

Tessy said – Basta! She made Anthony take her to the Oil Depot where in the back don Luca kept his office. She walked the last block so her grandson shouldn't get involved. She would take the car service home. The young man in the outer office was annoyed when she asked to be announced to don Luca. He might lose his place in his comic book. When don Luca himself came out, the young boob had respect on his face. Don Luca drew her into his inner office. Tessy nodded her head; outside was formica and girly calendars but inside was a palazzo, furniture you didn't get on Court Street. Don Luca made her sit on a soft leather sofa, one you didn't fall down into and then couldn't get up out of unaided like Carmella would have bought.

"Signora, you honor me. What service can we do for you?"

Tessy glanced at the hovering young man.

Don Luca said, "Bring coffee. Something. Go."

Don Luca, when he was young, without the title, worked on the docks with Tessy's husband before his 'accident'. He was maybe five years older than Tessy, no chicken but tall and straight with good hair and teeth. The suit he wore, mohair, you didn't see in this neighborhood. The young man brought wine, and anisette and almond cookies. He hovered. Don Luca looked at him. He went away.

Tessy said, "Don Luca, you and I are too old for formalities."

He smiled, "As the cart said to the horse: You go first."

"My son-in-law, Tony Fornucci. You and he do business. But this is a family thing; I hate to bother you. It's my daughter Carmella, I'm ashamed", she sniffled.

Don Luca took Tessy's hand, pursing his lips attentively. He knew when to be silent.

Tessy went on, "He's got a butana on the side. I say nothing. Men are goats. But this man beats up his wife too much. Once in a while we all understand. God knows she can't cook. But he's too much. Two, three times a week. Her nose doesn't know which way to turn. I can't turn a blind eye any longer. She's not a bad woman, a little stupido, that's all. One day he'll kill her. Help me."

Don Luca looked at the ceiling. He sighed. "Signora, you shame me. You show me the limits of my influence. In family affairs I can't interfere. It undermines the fabric of our society. If only there was another family member. If you had a son, he could step in. It would be proper. Nobody would side with Tony. But for me, in this I am powerless. She could leave him, no?"

Tessy sighed, looked at don Luca as if to say, she could grow another head, too.

"Anthony, your grandson?" he offered.

Tessy held up a hand, "It's not in him."

"Signora, my hands are tied. If it concerned business, I could step in. But..." don Luca held his palms up like the Pope.

Tessy's eyes narrowed. Business, she thought.

By some unseen summons the young man with the comic book appeared.

"Jimmy, get the car. You will take Signora Petrucci home or wherever she wishes."

He saw her out to the car. "Signora, I'm in complete agreement with you. Tony is not the apple of my eye, believe me. Ever since that trouble with your husband", he felt her elbow jerk under his guiding hand. He had said too much. He was getting old. He sighed, "The past is the past."

As don Luca seated Tessy in the limo, he said, "My only wish is that some day I may have the opportunity to show you I'm still a man before I die."

Tessy bowed her head with an old world grace. The car purred its way out of the yard in front of the Oil Depot. Tessy did not feel that she had come away completely empty-handed.

A few days later, Tessy received the gift in the mail from United Parcel, the tote bag from Channel 13 for her donation. The next day she received a duplicate by mistake. This started her thinking. The next Saturday she didn't make the gravy. She felt poorly. Carmella made the gravy. Tessy lay in her bed, smelling the gravy burning in the bottom of the pot as Carmella gabbed to a girlfriend on the phone. On Sunday she stayed in bed. All she would take was some broth. At the dinner table, from the open door, Tessy could hear even Anthony say, "Ma, what happened to the gravy?" Tony and Carmella went a few rounds and he slammed out of the house.

On Monday afternoon the two young men came with the bags of money. From the crack in her door, Tessy watched Tony and Carmella count the money and give the men a receipt. Anthony was away on an errand. After the men left, Tony and Carmella put the bundles of money in a large suitcase and simply stuck it behind the couch as usual.

Later, Tony took some of the money in an attaché case and went out on his rounds. Carmella went to her usual bingo game with her girlfriends. "Ma, if you want, I'll stay home. I'll make you some pastina." "No, no. I'm feeling much better." Anthony was at one of the arcades. Tessy was alone. She got dressed. She could be very swift and agile when she had a mission. She opened the suitcase and took out all the bundles of fifties, leaving the fives, tens and twenties. She stacked them into her Channel 13 tote bag. She took from the dryer the gym clothes Carmella had washed for Anthony and stuffed them into the second identical blue bag with the white straps. Tessy squeezed the second bag into the first bag. She lifted it. It was not heavy for a woman used to lifting heavy baskets of wet laundry, trays of lasagna and chicken cacciatore for a once large family, and to washing her own floors. Tessy called the car service she used when Carmella and Anthony weren't around. She stepped out on the porch. No one was around. She smashed the small glass panel near the door lock with her cane. She left the door closed but unlocked. Tessy made the car service drop her off at the pork store; then she walked the half block to the gym, the Adonis Health Club and Spa, where Anthony worked out. What was a Spa, anyway? She went in to where she knew the pay lockers were from other times. There were plenty of people there for a weekday, men and woman walking back and forth admiring themselves in floor length mirrors. Through a big window she could see the fools riding the bicycles that went nowhere. Mama Mia! Tessy said to herself, pick up a shovel. Do something useful! She opened one of the lockers and put the new blue bag inside.

A young man with muscles and a tee shirt with no sleeves came over, "Can I help you, lady?"

Tessy looked him up and down, "Who are you, Adonis?"

"I wish. You Okay?"

"Sure. Just leaving some clothes for my grandson, so he doesn't have to carry them around all day. He's a mailman. Capice?"

Adonis flexed his muscles, "Hey, mom, you want to work out?"

"I'll work you out with my cane, buffo", raising it menacingly above her head.

He danced away, "A tiger! A tiger! He went back to his magazine about vitamin supplements.

He'll remember me, nodded Tessy, pocketing the locker key.

Tessy went on her rounds. She bought braciole and veal at De Martino's for the scaloppini, then bread at Fasano's. Carmella would get the vegetables and the canned goods after bingo, things you could trust a child to do.

Tessy made a visit to St. Stephen's, conversing with God and Vincent, and loitering until she knew Carmella would get home and discover the broken windowpane. She could see her daughter running throughout the house calling, "Mama! Mama!" Then looking for the suitcase, finding it, relieved; then calling Tony at the Gloria Bowling Alley where he kept his office.

When the car service dropped Tessy home, Tony's big silver Caddy was half in the driveway and half on the sidewalk. She timed her arrival so that his first rage was over. She went in.

Tony had the stacks of bills spread out over the coffee table in the living room, counting them. Carmella was in tears, what else?

"What" said Tessy?

Carmella, her shopping bags at her feet, sobbed, "Somebody broke in. Look, the glass. They stole money."

Tessy dropped her bags, (nothing to break, anyway.) She threw her arms out like she had seen Maria Callas do on the TV, "Sona-ma-bitch! Call the police!"

Tony said, "Are you nuts? Shut her up."

Tessy hobbled to the kitchen, "my money in the kitchen. Carmella, see is it there, in the Medaglia D'Oro can behind the rice."

Carmella followed, "Mama, not your money. They didn't touch the house. The money in the suitcase, they took the money in the suitcase."

"But it's there. I saw it."

"Some of it, yeah. But the big stuff, the stacks of fifties they took."

"It had to be somebody who knew just where to go. And this used to be such a good neighborhood."

"It doesn't matter so much who took it. Tony still has to make it good."

"No. Go to don Luca. Tell him plain what happened. He'll understand. He knows Tony a long time."

Carmella shook her head, "Mom, make coffee, Okay? Stay here."

Carmella went back to the living room. Tony sat over the stacks of bills. He ran a damp handkerchief over his bald, sweating head, his wig on the table like a divot of sun burnt grass. He stared into the near distance, weighing his dwindling options.

Carmella leaned toward him, "So?"

"Over a hundred grand missing. All the fifties, there were twenty-two stacks of fifties in packs of one hundreds. That's one hundred and ten grand. Even if I had time to sell the boat, maybe one of the alleys, it's too late."

"Can you talk to don Luca?"

38

"We were never really close. He's been waiting for me to slip up."

"What about the money in the cellar?"

"That's only about twenty grand." He gave Carmella a withering stare. "I have to have it all distributed and accounted for by midnight. This is all your fault, you and that bitch of a mother of yours for leaving the house unattended. You know you're never supposed to leave the house when there's money here."

"Don't call my mother names."

Tony stood up shakily and backhanded Carmella onto the floor, "Get out of my sight, you fat bitch!" He pulled out a gun from his jacket pocket.

Carmella scrambled away and ran into the kitchen.

Tessy sat next to her sobbing daughter and cradled her head in her arms, "Shush, shush, everything will work out, Carmella. You'll see. Be quiet." She began to wonder if she hadn't over played her hand.

They heard the front door slam and rushed into the living room. Tony, the suitcase and the money were gone.

When Anthony got home his mother told him what she knew. He rushed around from bowling alley to arcade to bowling alley, discretely asking for his father. But still the word gets out that something is amiss. That night Carmella and Anthony tossed and turned. Tessy slept soundly.

The next morning, the two men who usually came on Mondays arrived, looking for Tony. One was Vic, the don's nephew. Carmella told of the broken glass, that Tony left around five p.m. Yes, he had the suitcase with him. No, he didn't say where he was going. As Tessy saw the men out she slipped a note to Vic with an address over in New York. From behind the window curtain, Tessy watched them drive off. She did not fail to notice the strange car down the street with two men in it reading the newspapers.

By Wednesday afternoon, Anthony's pacing and wringing of hands was driving Carmella crazy. Tessy made Anthony go down to the gym. "Take some exercise. You'll feel better. Here's the key for the locker. I left you clean clothes when I went to the pork store on Monday." Anthony was easily led by his grandmother.

Vic and his sidekick Nitty had ascertained that Tessy had taken car service to near the gym on Monday, carrying a gym bag of some sort, probably Channel 13. When Anthony left the house, a man in the car up the street called Vic on his cell phone. Vic and Ninny were waiting for Anthony when he arrived at the Adonis Spa. As Anthony opened the paid locker two other shadows merged with his.

Vic said, "Anthony, open the bag. Please."

They all looked into the bag,--underwear, a towel, no money. Nitty studied the interior of the small locker like it was the ceiling of the Sistine Chapel.

Vic said, "Let's go look at your regular locker in the locker room." They looked. Nothing.

Vic looked around the gym, "Anthony, knock yourself out."

"Vic, where's my father? What's happening?"

"He's your father. You tell us. If he calls in, you tell him the don wants to speak to him, capice?"

"Right."

Meanwhile, two men examined the apartment in Manhattan where Tony kept his butana. It was empty. Somebody had left in a hurry. But they had the make and model and license plate number of Tony's car.

Saturday morning in the papers, page five, a couple was found shot to death in a late model silver Cadillac at a truck stop on the Jersey Turnpike. Two 22's in the head for each of them. In the photo, the man's face was obscured by his toupee, which had fallen forward as his head lay against the steering wheel. Jewelry and cash were undisturbed. Robbery was ruled out. The shooting didn't get a lot of New York press because there were two other murders on Friday night in the city.

At the funeral, (closed coffin), Carmella sang grand opera and tore at her hair. Her bingo afficionadas gave her a '10'. But that night she ate two plates of linguine with oil and garlic. The don didn't show.

On the day of the burial, don Luca received a letter in the mail containing a key to a pay locker at the Adonis Spa. It was scotch taped to a blank, scented piece of note paper. He sent Vic to check it out. Vic noticed it was the locker next to the one Anthony had used. Inside was the other Channel 13 bag. Vic and don Luca examined the contents, $110,000.

By and by, don Luca called on Tessy while Carmella was at Bingo. He brought a small, pale yellow box tied with gold cord from a Little Italy patisserie. Tessy brought out a tray with coffee and the canneole, eclair and miniature napoleons the don had brought. Also a small bottle of anisette.

Don Luca said, "Please excuse my absence from the funeral. I meant no disrespect. But I no longer attend functions where the FBI will be taking pictures."

"We are all restricted in our choices in one way or another, no? Please, don Luca, take something."

They sipped demitasse, nibbled on biscotti.

The don said, "Tony was enrolled in an annuity plan. An envelope will arrive the first of each month for your daughter. But what can I do for you, signora?"

"My grandson, he is not cut out for this life of the bowling alleys. If you could find something for him in the country. Quiet. He was happiest when at camp."

"It shall be done."

"We thank you."

"Again, no offense intended for my absence from the funeral."

"None taken don Luca. Anyway, as you rightly reminded me in your office, it was a family affair".

FEAR

Fear moved slowly up Marion's arms and across the back of her neck. Reason fought with terror for her attention. She was, she reminded herself, a jogger, a good swimmer, even took karate. O.k., five years ago for three months. Here she was under the Manhattan end of the Brooklyn Bridge at eight at night with a flat, which she could have easily changed herself, but the spare was also flat.

Under the shadowy steel framework of the F.D.R. Drive there was a parking area, empty now on Friday night, its small white sentry booth locked and dark. This was February, windy and cold. In summer there would be some people about from the Fulton Fish Market and The South Street Seaport Museum. But she was three blocks north of the Market which at eight p.m. hadn't opened yet for its nocturnal labors. Much of South Street was still cobblestoned, littered with escaped hub caps, flattened mufflers, rags, beer cans and dead wine bottles. Used paper cups rolled in arcs across the street until coming to rest at the curb. The street light fifty feet away buzzed and stuttered, ready to go out.

Marion stood next to the driver's door surveying the jacked up rear end, open trunk, lug wrench and hub cap on the wet cobblestones. Her nails were gone. One suede shoe had a grease spot on it. She had the lights on and the flashes going, she left the door ajar to keep the interior light on for company.

She pulled her London Fog tightly around herself. A half block away was a pay phone she had walked to, to find the receiver had been torn away. No lights shown anywhere near her. She looked up at the Wall Street office buildings seven and eight blocks away,

43

many windows lit up, she envisioned the cleaning ladies listening to their favorite music stations as they vacuumed the rugs in the executive offices and board rooms.

Her office had no rug but the next one would. Friday nights she had to stay a little later in the bar with the boys to show them she was one of them; half of whom she rightly felt couldn't shine her shoes. It was a big law firm where jockeying for position went on all the time.

Lower Manhattan had emptied out by eight, commuters caught their trains to suburbia, others were at a show or in midtown hotels, bars and restaurants. 'Miss Independent' had to have her own car downtown. It was not the way to meet guys but made for fast getaways to the Hamptons or the slopes in season.

A low slung, white car came cruising slowly up South Street, and stopped next to her. The driver leaned over to her as his tinted window silently rolled down. From the dash lights she could see he was well dressed with gold chains, earrings and rings. He smiled, "What's happening, baby?"

She told him.

"Well climb in here, sugar. You can use my car phone to call AAA. And while they're fixing your boat you and me can get us a drink. Come on."

Marion bent down and picked up the jack handle and tapped his windshield with it. "Listen, Ace," she said evenly, "do you want to go for a new windshield and maybe a new head?"

"Nasty bitch!" he grunted and dug out leaving a cloud of exhaust and burnt rubber.

Marion heaved a sigh, she was shaking and perspiring but she felt good. She felt in control. She took a couple of deep breaths of the damp, salty air rolling off the East River. Under the Brooklyn side of the Bridge the Music Barge was all lit up but she could not hear the music. A large tug moved silently up the river, its running lights of red and green and three white ones on its mast, a small spotlight outlined the large black 'M' on the smoke stack. It pulled three barges of sand and gravel. She imagined them coming down the Hudson and now going out to Long Island to some small town on the north shore. Cars and trucks rumbled overhead on the F.D.R. A drain pipe above her leaked, rusty water splattering the cobblestones.

Where were the police cars she always saw cruising by, or the cabs, or the sanitation trucks, or the mail trucks, or Daily News and Post trucks? She searched her memory for the face of someone who would be missing her; her parents lived in Oneonta, her brother in California, she lived alone in her apartment on Sutton Place.

She had thrown Freddy out of her apartment and her life with a flair, with a flourish. He was a lizard but he had been her lizard. He would have missed her. He would have phoned her at the office, "Bring in some cigarettes, filters. Don't forget. And a bottle of Chivas Regal. And pick me up a copy of GQ. Don't be late, I'm hungry."

It was now 9:10. Traffic noises were growing fainter and less frequent. The wind began to howl up the canyoned streets from the Battery. The Music Barge looked so warm and inviting. She considered sitting in the car but didn't want to give up the visibility. Some civilized person had to come along, didn't they? She laughed to herself; if Freddy had been along she would still have had to change the flat herself. She seemed to have a thing for losers.

The wind died down. She could hear the hissing, sputtering street light again. She felt she was no longer alone. She turned towards the East River. Two men were emerging from the deep shadows cast by the Drive above. Her heart leapt in her breast! She tightened her grip on the jack handle.

They divided up, one coming around the rear and one around the front of her BMW. She began to raise the jack handle. They stopped. The one at the rear, lit yellowy by the flashing hazard lights, wore a dirty woolen hat pulled down over his ears. He had a black, caked and stained beard. She could not have said if he was black or white. He smiled to calm her, showing some teeth, none of them white. She stood where she could watch both of them.

Woolen Hat said, "We seen you. You got a flat. Want us to help you change it?"

"It's no use. The spare is flat also."

"We got a pump. Clarence, go get the pump." Clarence shuffled off to some crates silhouetted against the Brooklyn skyline. A chink of light escaped from one of them.

Don't the Police ever come by here? I've been standing here for over an hour."

"They come by after."

"After what?"

"After the fight. When there's a body. We'll pump up the spare. Sometimes it's just a slow leak. Then you can go to a gas station and get them both fixed. Sometimes it's just the valve needs to be changed. That's what me and Clarence do, fix flats. Collect hub caps, too. Bring them to the junkie. We seen that car that stopped. He's a pimp. See him all the time here."

Marion nodded, "He looked it."

46

"We would have come over sooner but we figured you called AAA. We don't like to come over if it's a woman. One screamed once and the cops came."

Clarence appeared with the bicycle pump at the rear and together they removed the spare and pumped it up.

"Looks good." said Woolen Hat as he squatted and deftly removed the loosened lug nuts from the wheel, removing it, rolling it away as Clarence rolled the spare into place. They mounted it and quickly spun home the lug nuts. Woolen Hat held out his hand for the jack handle, grinning, their eyes met. She gave him the handle. He tightened the nuts on the wheel, let down the jack and stowed it in the trunk. "Won't put the hub cap back on; only have to take it off at the gas station." he stood back, admiring his work.

"That was great. You guys are fast. What do I owe you?"

"Woolen Hat shrugged, "What ever you want. We really didn't fix the flat" he scratched himself; Clarence shuffled about in the cold, hugging himself.

Marion dug about in her bag. A small voice inside of her said, 'Share your lunch with them.', then an older voice said, 'Oh, get out of there while you're still in one piece.', then her mother, 'Ten is plenty!', then her grandmother, 'Do you think money grows on trees, missy?' She gave Woolen Hat a folded fifty. He didn't look at it, just clutched it. As she opened her door she almost said, 'Can I drop you anywhere?'

Woolen Hat said, "Well, we got to get back to our supper now. You be careful."

"You've really been very kind. Thanks a lot." God, she thought, when was the last time either of them received a Christmas card or a hug?

"Don't forget. Do both tires." They slipped away into the dark.

Marion got in, feeling her damp silk blouse press against her back as she sat back against the cold car seat. She turned off the hazard lights, locked all the doors twice and drove home. xxx

BILLY BARNACLE

On April 18th, Coast Guard Petty Officer 2nd class Alex Hamilton stationed at Key West, wrote his old 'Nam buddy, Billy McGonagle, now a Brooklyn Firefighter.

Dear Billy Barnacle,
How are you buddy? I am fine except going stir crazy down here in the Keys, now that summer is coming back. Already we are having days in the high 80's all the time with high humidity. It's the humidity that gets you like in 'Nam. We're all growing beards for something to do. Only interesting thing here was last month we were bringing in a derelict and we came across a cruiser, 40 footer, dead in the Straits - engine trouble. Two guys aboard knocked out from exposure. We took them in tow and called the station. We left Monte, a new guy, aboard our boat and me and Jimmy went aboard. Cubanos with bundles of queer American. That's why they couldn't call for help when their engine conked out. Me and Jimmy kept a pack of 5's and a pack of 1's to play poker with. You could spot the stuff a mile away, it's such lousy work. The plates must be pre-Castro. Who would be so dumb today to bother making 1's?
Now don't laugh. Am shipping over again next month. Hard to believe it's 12 years since we hooked up together on the Mekong Delta. I always wonder if I was right to stay in. How do you like being a fireman? I guess that's a hot job too. Ha Ha. When I ship over they have to give me a choice of duty station if there's an opening. I put in for Bar Harbor, Maine, a change of scenery from palms to pines. Have two new poker players down here and Jimmy

49

Robinson of course from 'Nam makes a fourth. Jimmy may go with me to Bar Harbor, and Monte Montenegro, a new guy from San Diego who is shipping over for the first time - fool! But he's a cool card player for a Mex. Jimmy says he never liked the food in those honky diners down here anyway and he wouldn't go into them if you paid him if it wasn't for the Civil Rights. One thing I learned in 'Nam - when they start shooting at your butt, we're all the same color. Jimmy says "Hello."

Will write again when I have the dates of my transfer. Will try to take a few days leave to stop by and visit on my way to Bar Harbor, if I get it, which I should. How is your father doing, now that he's retired? Say hello for me. He's a great guy. And Hello to Margie and little Billy Barnacle.

Your shipmate,
Alex.

p.s. Rosy still asking for you over at the Shalimar Café.

On April 24th, Billy replied.

Dear Alex,

Good to hear from you. Am doing fine on the Fire Department. I work with a lot of great guys here. As you can see we moved. Needed more room. It will be great if you and Jimmy can stop off on your way to Bar Harbor. Pop wants to drink you under the table again like he did at my wedding. My son, (4 yrs. old on Mar 4th.), we call him William with pop and me both Bill.

News! Picked up an old cabin cruiser cheap in a boat yard, a Wheeler 30'. Am having the guy I bought it off, Robby Morgan who owns the yard, caulk it and fix it up for me. With the second job I don't have time to do it myself. I help a guy paint houses on the side. There was a Criss-Craft 35' with a flying bridge, all chrome and teak decks and two fighting chairs I had my eye on but Robby wanted $19,000. for it. Too much for me. Can't wait to get out fishing on the briny. Pop knows all the good spots between Long Island and Jersey. Maybe you and Jim can get to go with us if you're in town. Boy, will it feel good to get a deck under my feet again. Margie says hello, "You should find a nice girl and settle down."

I miss the Guard but Marge and William more than make up for it. Wouldn't have it any other way. Eight years was enough.

Pop had to let his boat go when I was in because the arthritis got so bad he couldn't handle the boat. It will be good to get him out on the water again.

Well, have to go to work.

Hang in, swabby,
Billy

On May 8th, Billy's father, Bill, Sr. wrote Alex at Key West.

Dear Alex,

Just a few lines to let you know Billy had an accident with that damn boat of his. He's in the hospital with exposure. He's o.k. The doctor says a week or so and he can come home. He went out fishing over by Sandy Hook and got caught in a squall. The boat sprung a hundred leaks in the twisting and turning and on top of that the new bilge pump he had installed broke down and anyway, the boat sunk. Billy had to hang on to the gun'all for hours. Finally a fisherman from Red Bank N.J. spotted him and brought him in.

He's down in the dumps over the boat. I say good riddance to bad rubbish. It was a piece of junk. Better this way than if he had the boy with him. That Morgan has no morals selling a wreck like that. Billy wouldn't but I called the Police. They put me onto the Better Business Bureau. They said there was nothing they could do since Billy didn't have a bill of sale for the caulking and the bilge pump which if I know that crook Morgan like I do wasn't new anyway. He paid Morgan $3,000. for that old Wheeler. Must be 50 years old. He should be arrested. They said they had other complaints against him but he always has a lawyer with him. I told Billy to write you but he is too depressed. I don't believe he even caulked that wreck, just smeared some cheap paint on the hull. Billy is too trusting like his mother. That's why I'm writing.

Well, take care of yourself,
Bill, Sr.

On May 11th, Alex wrote Billy.

Dear Bill

Had a note from your father. Sorry to hear about your boat. That guy Morgan sounds like a real creep. Don't worry; those guys get theirs in the end. If I remember right, isn't that the guy who sold us the spoilt bait that time your pop took me fishing? I remember that place now, an old barge. I wrote my brother George the Treasury Agent who works in the section where they auction off confiscated boats and planes that were seized from dope smugglers. I gave him your address, asked if he couldn't let you know when the next auction was and if he could keep an eye open for you for a nice boat.

Don't get depressed. We were in worse trouble when our boat hit that mine in the Mekong River. I thought we were goners. But we made it back through the jungle. And you carrying me half the way when my leg swole up like a balloon. I will never forget it. I owe you, buddy. One good thing about letters is you can't tell me to shut up. I got the Purple Heart and you got the bad back.

Well, my transfer came through. And Jimmy and Monte too. You should see our beards. Even Jimmy's is o.k. Monte has a Poncho Villa moustache, too. But mine is the longest, bushy really. You wouldn't know me. I will try to send you a picture. They won't give us no leave as we all used up our Annual for this year. They are flying us up to Bar Harbor to be in time for a class that's starting 6/03 on a new patrol boat we have to learn all about. We leave on June 1st. The class is six weeks. After that we maybe can get together. Say hello to pop and Margie and li'l Bill. Jimmy and Monte and Rosy say hello.

So long for now,
Your shipmate Alex

On June 5th, Billy replied.

Dear Alex,
Read the enclosed clipping later for all the details, but do I have news! The cops raided Robby Morgan's boat yard on Memorial Day and found all kinds of stolen stuff, boats, ship-to-shore radios, depth finders, marine batteries, you name it. And counterfeit money, too! That's what put them on to him. Phony ones and fives started showing up in the neighborhood and they traced them to the boat yard. It was the money that got the Feds involved and they

got search warrants to examine the whole premises and came down on him like gang busters. They arraigned him at Central Booking in Brooklyn. It was on the T.V. His lawyer, another sleaze, said Mr. Morgan didn't know the depth finders and radios were stolen. He acted in good faith - $800 dollar depth finders he paid $200 for! Then sold for $400. or $500! They're going over all his records and income tax returns.

Your brother called and said Morgan's stuff would be auctioned off by the Treasury Dept, if he's convicted of course. He will call and let me know when it is. He asked if there was anything I liked. I said I'd like to get a hold of that Criss-Craft I told you about but that $19,000. was way over my head. He said he thought it would go at about $1,500!!! The government isn't in the boat business, he said.

The guy on the T.V. news said the counterfeiting was the worse rap. Morgan's lawyer tried to shut him up but he said he was clean on the funny money, trying to cop a plea. He said a black guy came in to the yard the day before Memorial Day and bought a rusty old anchor off him for $20. He paid in fives and ones. He said he would pick it up the next day. Then a Puerto Rican comes in, in the afternoon and buys the same anchor for $30. and says he will be back in the morning with his truck. Morgan moves the anchor across the yard in case the black guy comes back. He'll say there was a mix up and give him his twenty bucks back. Now his lawyer practically has his hand on Morgan's mouth. The T.V. loved it. Morgan says, no, he has nothing to hide. Then he said this white guy with a big cowboy hat and a red beard, a rebel he says, comes in, in a fancy car. Says he's an antique dealer looking for old anchors and stuff to landscape the front of a new restaurant out in the Hamptons, out on Long Island. Ritzy neighborhood. What about that old anchor over there, says the guy with the beard? Sold, says Morgan. Too bad says Red Beard. I can go maybe 90 to 95 bucks for it. Morgan says o.k. His lawyer says he's under a strain.

Then the guy pulls out a check book. Morgan says no checks. He got stuck too many times. Believe that? Strictly cash and carry. The guy paid for the anchor with a stack of fives. None of them ever came back for the anchor. The young assistant D.A. on the steps says he hopes Mr. Morgan tells that story in court. It was a conspiracy, Morgan says. But he could identify them all for sure as long as they don't shave off their beards. When asked what effort would be made to find the three men, the police captain said it would be like looking for a needle in a haystack. If they did exist, they probably shaved their beards off by now, if they were real, he said. It's not often you see the cops laughing on the T.V.

Will they let you three keep your beards up at Bar Harbor? Well, guess that's all for now. Write when you can get some leave. I go on vacation in August. Maybe Marge and William and pop and me will drive up to Bar Harbor and go camping. We can all go out fishing, maybe.

Your shipmate,
Billy Barnacle
p.s. Tell Jimmy and Monte hello.
p.p.s. And I don't want to hear about the Mekong anymore.

"C-A-T, Cat"

Virginia, 185_

The Major stood at the window of the breakfast room watching the surrey descend the drive, passing the stately row of oaks to the road to Richmond; old Nathan with his battered top hat, driving, Mrs. Major and the tutor, Miss de Haviland on the next seat with their silly little parasols that wouldn't shade a frog, and Auntie Bell, the cook with her go-to-town head scarf on the back bench.

The Major's linen napkin slid down his stained vest onto the polished plank floor, forgotten. He cocked his head, the house was quiet. Auntie Bell's pots and pans were quiet in the kitchen. His wife's desk was quiet. She was forever rattling bills and letters, dropping account books on the floor, ringing her little bell for Sissy. Always accusing him of spending more than they took in, whatever that meant. Only reason he allowed her to do the accounts was to give her something to do to get her to stop moping around the house, with the girls gone and such.

He started to shout, "Sis...", when she appeared in the doorway with an empty tray. "Oh, Sissy."

"Yessir."

"Where's that rascal Jerome at to this morning?"

"Auntie Bell set him to dustin' the books, sir."

"Ah, yes the books."

Sissy gathered up the breakfast things and slid out of the room. The Major thought, I could swear that bitch has casters for feet. Never makes a sound. Maybe I should put bells around their necks.

Jerome and the books. The Major had been suspicious of Jerome for some time. He was found in the library most every day. Did books need dusting every day? The Major treaded silently down the hall to the library in his worn slippers. He prided himself on never having read a book on his shelves, bought them by the pound from England. The door was ajar. He peeked through the crack. He could see a sliver of Jerome standing with an open volume in one palm and a duster in the other. Was he daydreaming or reading? Today would be a good day to find out with her ladyship and that Yankee tutor, and Auntie Bell off in town for the day. Tutor! Had to get all grand and learn French. Most sissified talk he ever did hear. That would be his next project; getting rid of that meddlesome Yankee tramp, Miss de Haviland, always saying 'Thank you.' to Sissy and Jerome when they put the plates on the table like they was quality. Talking about Christianity and morale. Morale came at the end of his boot. Daddy would turn over in his grave if he could hear such trash. I bet they'll be a lot less dusting of books after she's gone.

The Major pushed open the tall door. It squeaked. Jerome flinched and closed the book.

"Why you got that book open? You dusting every page, fool?"

"Nosir. I dropped it." Jerome hung his head and slid the thick book back onto the shelf.

The Major squinted at the spine of the book, "Fool. You put it back upside down. Turn it around. Turn it around."

Jerome was rattled. He slid the book off the shelf, and looking at the Major for guidance turned the book so the spine faced the wall.

"No, you fool!" the Major grabbed the book and replaced it correctly. "Nobody can see the title that way." The Major shook his head; they're too dumb for words.

He sat at his desk and took out pen and paper. "Come over here, Jerome". Jerome limped over and stood penitently at the desk. The Major put on his spectacles and dipped his quill into the inkwell. He scratched out a brief note, looking up to see if Jerome was watching him. Jerome stood, eyes downcast, shoulders slumped, one heel in the air to keep his back straight. The Major waved the note in the air to dry the ink, then folded it once, lightly. He turned in his chair to look out the large window. Beyond was a large kitchen garden, maybe thirty yards wide by a hundred deep. Running down one side was a shady grape arbor. At the far end was a row of peach trees. Beyond the trees, he could see Mr. Flint, the overseer. He had some boys cutting and clearing brush.

The Major looked up at Jerome's one blue eye and one brown eye. He wondered from time to time about some of his people of a certain age; was they his seed from a night of carousing with a jug in a corncrib? Naw, all too dumb to have any white blood in them.

"Jerome, take this note out to Mr. Flint, you hear?"

"Yessir." Jerome took the note and slouching, hobbled from the room.

"Sissy!"

Sissy appeared, "Yessir."

"Why does Auntie Bell keep that fool, Jerome in the house? I'd sell him down river if I could get a buyer for a cripple. But nobody wants him."

"Auntie Bell, she say Jerome the only one can knead the bread dough like she do since her hands all gone crooked."

"What about you?"

"Auntie Bell, she say I don't got the touch."

"He do the cornbread, too?"

"Yessir."

"Best cornbread on the James, some folks say."

"Yessir."

Major nodded and Sissy left. Still, he thought, can't have them readin' an' writin'. No telling where it would lead. Always gave me a headache. Can't see the point of it. Daddy always said all a man really needs is a gun and some good hounds.

The Major missed his two daughters away in that finishing school in Baltimore; their running and screaming in delight up and down the halls, especially on rainy days. When his son died and the doctor said she couldn't have any more, they drifted apart. Boy was too young for that horse, she said. He was eight. I was riding when I was five. Just plain bad luck.

He looked out the window. The sun was topping the trees and picking out the tomatoes and peppers. The long grape arbor appeared in even darker shade. He couldn't see Jerome but knew just about where he'd be. If Jerome could read, he couldn't resist looking at the note, and if he read it he'd be getting ready to run like the devil was onto him. Oh, he wouldn't get far with that short leg, but they never learn.

Jerome slowed his pace under the thankful shade of the grape arbor. He looked around cautiously. He could hear the rhythmic chopping of the machetes. He delicately unfolded the note and moving his lips, read,

"Flint – Send those boys down to the river to stack wood. Have Jerome dig a trash pit where you are at behind the peach trees; then shoot this nigger and dump him in it. You cover him. We'll say he run off. M."

Jerome blinked and read again. He folded the note. He looked up at the shadowy canopy of grape leaves, the green sun boring through the lacy edges and outlining the veins of the broad leaves, his breathing quickening. He swallowed hard. He took a stance as if about to bolt. Then he passed a hand across his forehead. He couldn't have put a name to it but he was reasoning, weighing options. Was this a test to see if he could read? Bait for the fox? If he kept on to Mr. Flint, he'd be dead before suppertime. Oh, he knew the Major hated him special. And if he run, the Major, he know for sure who taught him to spell cat, Miss 'Lizabet. Ever'body knew it against the law for white folk to teach darkies to read. She could maybe go to jail. Jerome could see Miss 'Lizabet in chains in a dungeon. His head began to ache. This was all happening like Miss 'Lizabet said it might. She said reading was like fire; could be friendly or could be hurtful, that there was a price to pay for learnin'. "Responsi- responsib-", he couldn't rightly pronounce the long word, responsibility yet. Jerome had believed that anything in a book was gospel. She say lying in books was worse than saying it 'cause it lasted longer and most people believed everything they read.

Nobody run off in daytime. If you run, fool, run at night and follow that star, the North Star. Put some food in your pocket. Run up and down every stream you cross. Maybe throw the dogs off for a time and run 'til your heart burst. Amos, he run last winter after Major whip him. He could run like a deer but they catch him. Beat him fearful. Now Amos just stare. No light behind his eyes. They like windows in an empty house, nobody in there to look out. Mr. Flint bring you back dead or alive. Must be a long way to Pennsavany, like the Promised Land, just too far to touch.

Jerome came to an arch in the side of the arbor. He could step out here and trot into the woods. Pretend he free for a couple of days.

Major called out, "Sissy, any of that cornbread left?"

"Yessir."

"Bring me some. Put plenty of 'lasses on it, hear."

"Yessir." Sissy glided away.

Jerome thought, if the Mrs. knew what he was about, she'd say he was cutting off his nose to spite his face. Learning, Miss. 'Lizabet say is the slow unfolding of a treasure map to knowledge, a treasure that they can't take away from you. And you can't lose it. It won't guarantee happiness, whatever that is; but it will explain away some of the pain and ignorance and doubt.

Learning the letters and seeing how to make 'cat' was a joy, sweet like the first rain after the heat wave. Then the frowning over longer words like 'all men are created equal', 'pursuit of happiness'. Jerome had been amazed that Miss 'Lizabet knew who her pap's pap was. "Jerome, if you were a hunting dog or a horse, the Major would have a record of your mammy and pap, and their mammies and paps." Who is my pap? How old am I? Why am I black? It slowly dawned on Jerome what was happening, what was different. He had been given the ability to examine the world around him and make a decision. He never made a decision in his life. Every movement he made, every morsel he ate was decided for him, if not by the Major then by the rising and setting of the sun. Other questions flitted across his mind; if there be only one Promised Land, why did we need two different graveyards?

Jerome stepped into the sunlight, shuffled over to Mr. Flint and proffered the folded note from the Major.

Mr. Flint scratched an ear, now what? He read the note, looked up at Jerome and reread it. He looked off towards the house and shook his head.

After Jerome got into the rhythm of digging, he could almost forget what he was doing. The sweating felt good. And nobody could see you thinking. Flint sat in the shade on a crate watching Jerome. He wiped his neck with an old bandana, calculating the depth of the hole Jerome was vigorously digging. The Major was a fool, like all of them that never did a lick. You didn't kill off good property, like burning cotton 'cause you didn't get your price. A taste of the cat did for most of the uppityness. What was the Major's complaint with this boy? No prize with that limp but you never had to go looking for him like some of them. Some blacks said there was voodoo in him with that one blue eye.

Jerome was down past his waist now. Never once paused. Flint stood and drew his revolver. He spun the cylinder and squinted at the house.

Sissy waited while Major cleaned the plate of the cornbread, wiping up the last drops of 'lasses with the crumbs. He licked his fingers. She looked out the window at Jerome digging and the height of the sun above his glistening back, like black marble.

"Mr. Major, sir."

"What?"

"Auntie Bell say she want Jerome to start on the dough mixin' and breadin' of the chicken for dinner now, when the sun high."

"Does she, Sissy?"

"Yessir."

"Auntie Bell don't run this farm, does she?"

"Yessir, Nosir." Poor Sissy didn't know whether to move her head from side to side or up and down.

"Maybe we'll have to eat that leftover ham tonight." he laughed softly.

"Yessir. Mrs. Major, she say she want dinner on the table when she step down off the surrey. Mrs. Major get powerful hungry from being in town."

The Major scratched his head through his thinning reddish hair; maybe this wasn't the best day for this scheme. He looked out the window. He could just see Jerome's shoulders and head. He scribbled a note.

"Sissy, run this note out to Mr. Flint."

"Yessir."

Sissy was glad to get out of the house and have an excuse for a leisurely stroll under the long shady arbor. She plucked a broad grape leaf and fanned herself grandly as she had seen Mrs. Major do with her fan from France when company come.

Flint's shadow loomed over Jerome. "That's deep enough, Jerome. Throw up the shovel."

Jerome straightened his back to Flint. He glanced off at the rows of lettuce, level with his eyes. The pearls of dew still nestled in the folds of the green leaves.

Flint raised his pistol as Sissy emerged from the arbor.

"Mr. Flint, sir." she waved the note.

Flint said, "Jerome, come up out of there. Go wash up and get over to the kitchen with Sissy."

"Yessir."

As Jerome sluiced himself with the tepid water from the horse trough, he thought about the books. Must be some magic in them the white man was afraid they'd learn. Still, it was all very dangerous. Maybe he should stop. But he knew he wouldn't. He

63

could take a book and hide it, and read it at night and on Sunday when the white folk were in church. It was like taking a griddle cake off the fire behind Auntie Bell's back; you knew your fingers would get burnt but still. He'd get a piece of candle from the kitchen drawer. But then someone was bound to see him. Would they turn him in? Or would he read to them, then the letters, then 'cat'. Even if they killed him, they couldn't stop this thing, like wild fire. Like Miss 'Lizabet say, "Knowledge is power."

Jerome knew if your hands were busy, they had no inkling you were thinking. He dried himself with his tattered shirt and put it on. He limped back to the kitchen, head bent, a new light in his eyes.

Baltimore, MD, 186-
READ
First words are beginning draughts we take,
For a thirst the wise find hard to slake,
To build a world lies scarce can hide in,
Read and see your options widen,
As well as newly minted pages,
Scan the tomes of ancient sages,
Come see life's secret skein unravel,
For books are silk routes our mind's eye travel.
Jerome Major   XXX

The Blue Sweater

Many long years ago when I was in my last year of Medical School I boarded with Mrs. Murphy. There were only three of us. I with my small dog, Spot, old Mr. Kovkosski who played third violin in the local orchestra, and Miss Fallon the music teacher, each banned from other boarding houses for our eccentricities. Most boarding houses wouldn't allow dogs, Mr. Kovkosski would rise in the middle of the night and begin sawing away at the magnum opus he had been composing for twenty years, Miss Fallon used the parlor to teach voice and piano to tone deaf local louts who could have saved their poor parents the fees and been doing useful work in the lumber mill.

Mrs. Murphy's cooking made me long for those devastating colds that took ones appetite away for weeks. The rooms were small and dreary. There was no central heating. The one ray of sunshine was Mrs. Murphy's beautiful daughter, Doris. In the mornings, Doris helped her mother set culinary history back for decades in the kitchen. When I would return from classes, she would be sitting in the parlor knitting away. Sometimes a local beau would be in tow with ukulele or his own piano sheet music after Miss Fallon had allowed the piano to cool off. I saw in the parlor and the knitting the metaphor of the spider and the fly and gave no encouragement to Doris. Her mother never gave up hope of calling me 'son'. She did my laundry, taking pains to iron the collars and cuffs neatly even though she sheared off many useful buttons. When we ate, Mr Kovkosski, straining his watery soup through his drooping mustache and Miss Fallon sitting so erect would fix their beady eyes on my plate which would always seem to have more meat on it than theirs. Meat which I always believed had gotten closer to a saddle than I ever would.

But I must say, Doris was always friendly without being coquettish. She could converse on the popular topics of the day and the latest books, more so than I with my nose always in textbooks. Doris was kind enough to take Spot out every day for me while I was away at school. One day as the holiday season approached, Mrs Murphy casually asked what my favorite color was. Blue, I said and forgot the incident. I suppose with my schooling ending the following spring, the Murphys thought to turn up the heat. I sensed that Mrs. Murphy was urging Doris to be more forward and contrived for Doris and me to be thrown together. Of course I was flattered but I saw myself wending my way down life's highway in tandem with more of a thoroughbred than Doris. How fortunate for the public that I knew more of medicine than of women.

In early December, I returned from a dreary lab session well after dinnertime to my warmed plate at the back of the coal stove. Doris was still at her knitting or should I say station. She swept away what she was working on but not before I was allowed ample time to see that it was of blue wool. As I ate my supper she kept me company. In the glow of the gas lamp her hair shined like copper shavings off a lathe, her eyes were very blue. Why had I not noticed before?

At odd moments I would speculate about the sweater Doris was knitting for me, would it have a collar, sleeves or no? Would it be double breasted with big brass buttons? There was no question of a present from me, a poor medical student.

On Christmas morning, Spot wagged his tail and scratched at my bedroom door to get out. He sensed something special in the air this day. I paid careful attention to dressing, being sure to wear no vest or sweater. I walked leisurely down the stairs, well pleased with my appearance.

In the parlor Mrs. Murphy, Miss Fallon, and Mr. Kovkosski were all standing around the small Christmas tree laughing and exchanging Seasons Greetings. Although their backs hid Spot from my view I could hear his happy little bark. He was obviously entertaining everyone with one of the tricks I had taught him. I could not see Doris. They all turned and parted at my cheery Christmas greetings to one and all. I stopped short. There was Spot wearing a new blue wool coat with brass buttons and his name embroidered on the side. "Look at the beautiful coat Doris made for Spot." said Miss. Fallon, laughing. "Like a prince he looks." said Mr. Kovkosski, cackling into his beard. "Where's Doris?" I said, looking about me. Mrs. Murphy said, "Oh, she's up and out a long time. Gone ice skating with Harry the mayor's son. Merry Christmas. son

FINER FEELINGS

Buster Stone headed his 98 Nissan through the construction bottleneck that held traffic to a crawl on the Shore Parkway, on his way to J.F.K. to pick up his wife, Maureen. He checked his watch and returned to drumming his fingers on the steering wheel. He had forgotten to bring any tapes. There was nothing any good on the radio. He had to take a piss. He knew he should have gone before he left the saloon. He rolled down the window for a little fresh air. He knew he shouldn't have let Steve and Ralph talk him into that last game of pool at the Do Drop Inn. But what were Saturdays for? They were rare enough where you could shoot a couple of games of pool with your friends and quaff a few brews. Being a fireman for Buster was sometimes like walking through life on one side of a picket fence while all your friends were on the other side; you saw them part of the time and even when you couldn't see them, you knew what they were doing only you couldn't be a part of it, not when you only got a full weekend off about once a month. On a week day in the Do Drop all you saw were old retired guys and bums. While most people's social life revolved around the weekends, a fireman had to make something up for himself from Monday to Friday. He couldn't take his kids to play ball in the park or fishing if school was in session.

Now he was afraid he was going to be late for Maureen's plane. He glared at his watch as if to retard the hands. It was 5:16. She was due in on the 6:15 from Chicago where she had been visiting her sister Alice. Mike, his brother-in-law worked for a big outfit that relocated them to Chicago. Twenty-one years he worked for them. It was move or start looking for another job. Start all over again at forty-two! Buster didn't think he could do it. Not after fifteen years on the Fire Department.

The Fire Department was a strange mixture of boredom and excitement. After you got used to the weird hours and the quick change up of the job; one minute you're cleaning a toilet bowl in the bathroom and the next you're inching your way down a smoky hallway on your knees, where the temperature just over your head is 300 degrees and you're dying to open the nozzle but you know you can't because the fire is down the end of the hall and around a corner in a kid's bedroom and opening the nozzle prematurely will not put out one inch of fire but make searing steam as it hits the hot plaster walls. Steam can do a worse job on you than fire because you're not as quick to pull away from it. And the fire was always on the third floor, rear. Buster hadn't even bothered to shower after he got off duty at nine this morning. He had driven straight to the Do Drop, it being Saturday and all. When he got there a softball team was gathering before they went to the field. He had a beer, like a sponge he absorbed it. He could still smell the smoke in his hair, remembering how Feeney from the truck had fallen through the floor in front of him. Right in front of him; the floor gave way, the fire came up and grabbed Nick and pulled him down, like into hell. They got him out. Chopper landed right in the meadow in Prospect Park and took him right up to the Cornell Burn Unit. Somebody said his fingers were gone. If he didn't have the mask on he would have been long gone. That's why Buster didn't go home; the house was empty. He had to be around people; specially people who hadn't been at the fire. People who complained about parking and orthodontia.

It sounded like everyone behind Buster was blowing his horn at him. They were. The traffic was moving and there was a big gap between him and the cars in front of him. He should have taken a six pack with him. He figured he'd piss in his pants just about the time he got to the parking lot.

How many times had he been told; don't take the job home with you. But you had to unwind slowly or wake up in the middle of the night, sweating, your heart going like a trip hammer. Buster had called the firehouse twice from the Do Drop but there was no word. It could have been me. Why wasn't it me?

5:30. Hey, what if Maureen's early? Then he's got to listen to another lecture about punctuality. Why didn't he call the airline to see if the flight was on time? Why didn't he leave earlier? Why couldn't he stay out of the bars for one morning? Because he just couldn't get enough of poplar tree roots clogging drainpipes and grubs turning lawns brown. Traffic stopped again. 5:40. It seems they've been working on this section of the Parkway for years. When the hell are they going to be finished? Moving again.

He and Maureen had found out a week ago that her sister Alice had split with Mike. He wondered what old Mike was doing or who in his new pad. He knew what he'd be doing. Big sister Maureen of course had to fly out and hold Alice's hand. She had more time for that social climbing bitch than for him.

Buster found a parking spot near American Airlines and dashed in. It was 18:05 hours. He scanned the TV monitors, searching the arrivals column. Maureen's flight was #462 from Chicago. In the column where it usually says, "ARRIVED" or "ON TIME" it said "DELAYED" and the new arrival time was 19:10. Buster calculated; that's a fifty-five minute delay. He looked at his watch; 6:10. That's an hour from now, damn! He busted his ass getting here for nothing. Should have called the airline.

Buster looked around at the people scurrying back and forth. A large arched window looked out on two parked planes; food and luggage were being stowed onboard. Two men with ear protectors and clipboards were examining the landing gear as if to advertise; hey, are we safety conscious or what? This window dressing reminded Buster of the restaurant his parents had taken him to in Manhattan where you could watch the chefs preparing the meal through a glass partition. His mother had said that's to show you how clean the kitchen is. It wasn't till then that Buster suspected that it could have been otherwise. Only he and a small boy were looking down on the oil stained maintenance bays. Large portable, red painted foam extinguishers stood around the area like Coldstream Guards. Two baggage handlers stood smoking under the "NO SMOKING" sign in three languages.

Buster stopped at a phone booth and called the firehouse. Lonny, a chauffeur answered, "A Chaplain took his wife up to the Burn Center. He's in a coma. It looks bad. A lot of third degree. His crotch. There's no protection there. Costello went up there. He'll stay till something happens. We'll pray. What else can you do?"

Buster walked into the glassed-in restaurant, under the arched sign, "Cuisine of the Clouds". It was crowded. Saturday was always a busy day at the airport. He got himself a burger and a Bud. All the tables were taken. He walked around them with his tray. At the end of the room, in a corner, was a table with a couple seated behind it on the upholstered couch that ran along the wall.

He said, "Do you mind if I sit down? It's pretty crowded." smiling in his winning way.

They seemed surprised to be spoken to, not annoyed. The woman smiled brightly. They were dressed in their Sunday best. The woman was thin and plain. She clung lightly to his arm. The man was broad shouldered; his face and hands tan from outdoor work.

"Sure. Have a seat."

Buster noticed that they had had the stew and were finishing desert.

Having made many trips to J.F.K. over the years, Buster had long ago concluded that the molded plastic seats in these places must have been designed by the prankster son of a hard nosed farmer; determined that the city slickers should know what it felt like to sit on a cold, hard tractor seat. He could tell these two didn't frequent airports. They had tried to make a pleasant meal of airport food. They hadn't finished their plates. A crumbling muffin sat before the woman while he continued to toy with a soggy wedge of apple pie.

Buster knew that if he had any more to drink without eating, he'd be drunk and started munching on his burger. It was greasy and cold. God knows how long it lay floating in that tray waiting for him, he thought.

Buster grinned with his mouth half full, an amber crescent of onion dangling from his lower lip. If his sainted mother were present she would slap him silly.

"They should be arrested," he mumbled, "for passing this off for food. And we should be committed for eating it."

They could not take their eyes off the piece of onion. She smiled shyly.

Now that he had so much time to kill, Buster was unwinding, eager to talk. "Here to pick up my wife. Coming in from Chicago. Visiting her sister. Due in at six-fifteen. I race out here. What happens? Plane's going to be an hour late."

Leaning forward anxiously, the woman said, "Oh, I hope everything's all right. What is it, a storm?" She searched the sky for trouble.

"Nothing so dramatic. What they do is hold up the plane for some connecting flight from Denver or LA or San Francisco. You see," Buster took a swallow of beer, some of it dribbling down his chin, "a lot of the people from the coast and Hawaii are trying to make connections at Kennedy for England and Europe. The European flights all leave at about either ten in the morning or seven-thirty, eight-thirty at night. The New York-Chicago run is almost like a shuttle. Like New York to D.C. or Boston, see?" Buster took another long swallow, warming to his subject. He had the airlines all figured out, like some people do the weather.

Sitting close together, the couple nodded politely, frowning, trying to hang onto the thread of Buster's tale.

He went on, "If they don't make the connecting flight at Kennedy for Europe the airline has to pay the hotel bill for the passengers for tonight and then put them on the morning flight. The planes to Europe don't wait. The tourist industry is a big lobby. They tell their customers tomorrow is their first day in England or France and they better be there. They don't care if they inconvenience a few people in Chicago. It's not like tomorrow was a business day. Get it? But they better get those first class

73

passengers and their tourist packages where they want to be on time. Get it?"

For the couple behind the table, Buster's monologue, like the stew was not completely digestible. They began to wonder how these revelations could affect their flight plans. The man looked down at his wristwatch, then reassuringly smiled at the woman, squeezing her hand.

During this pause, Buster took another bite of his burger. The crescent onion fell from his lip and monogrammed his yellow sports shirt. At first, Buster had taken these two for a boss and his secretary off for a junket in the islands, but then he noticed how relatively formal they were dressed; he in a gray suit and red tie, she in a nice blue suit beneath her new raincoat. She wore an old tortoise shell broach at the neck of her white lace blouse. She wore old-fashioned dark rimmed eyeglasses that made her look planer than Buster suspected she was. She looked about thirty-five, he in his fifties.

Buster said, "Where you off to, Jamaica?"

"Oh, no." the man answered quickly, as if Jamaica were too exotic or distant. "Bermuda."

"Bermuda" Buster smiled, nodding his head. "Beautiful place. You're going to love it. Went there on my honeymoon."

The couple leaned forward, smiling eagerly. The man said, "How is it this time of year? Not too cold, I hope. We weren't sure. We haven't done much traveling.

Buster nodded at the corsage, "Anniversary?"

The woman clutched the man's sleeve, suppressing a giggle, saying, "Oh, I knew I should have taken it off."

74

"No." the man chided, turning a little red in the face. Then to Buster, "We just got married this morning."

Buster looked from one to the other, grinning foolishly. He was maintaining his buzz from the Do Drop. Then extending his hand and knocking over the napkin dispenser, "Oh, congratulations. Buster Stone."

Hesitantly, the man shook hands. Buster noticed he had a powerful grip. "Thank you." he smiled shyly bending his head and withdrawing his hand. "Fred Flegenshorn."

The woman reached towards Buster, "Helen Hooley. Oh, I'm so nervous. I mean, Helen Flegenshorn." she corrected, looking lovingly at Fred, then back at Buster as he shook her hand. "Is this a good time to go to Bermuda? I mean, it's still so cold here in New York."

"This is the best time of the whole year to go." Buster waved a hand, knocking over his beer can, catching it before it could roll off the table. "You get to appreciate the contrast more. See how it is here, only a few buds on the trees, cold rain all the time, mud. In Bermuda it's like two months ahead, like June, say. Not too hot, not too cool. Everything's in bloom. Flowers all over. They have a beautiful flower down there called the Passionflower. It has a very strong scent. You can smell it all over the island. They have a perfume factory, too. They make their own perfume. Only drawback is the ocean is still too cold in April to swim in. Looks inviting though. You can see right to the bottom but it's like ice water."

"Oh, I don't think we'll be doing much swimming." Helen said rather wistfully.

"They got pools, though," defended Buster, sounding like a tourist agent, even to himself but he couldn't stop. His own honeymoon came flooding back to him like a batch of snapshots that hadn't faded over the last fourteen years. 'Oh, this place is so beautiful; we have to come back some time.' "The pools are heated plus the sun. But the best thing is the motor bikes. It's the best way to see the island."

Fred said, "The brochure says they have horse and buggies."

"Oh, yeah. But they're so slow. Takes all day to get anywhere."

Helen patted Fred's arm; "We're in no hurry."

Buster was rolling his empty beer can between his sweaty palms, "How long you going for?"

"Two weeks. Two whole weeks." Helen brightened at the prospect.

"Two weeks! That's great. You must have a nice boss."

"Fred's the boss." Helen said, hugging his arm.

Fred turned to her shyly, "You're the boss now."

Helen burst out; "You know those little green newsstands you see all over town?"

"Yeah." The thirst was upon Buster.

"Well, Fred invented them."

"Oh, Helen." Fred whispered modestly.

"And he has a patent, too. The 'Quick-Erect Stand.' with the double roof."

Buster smiled in admiration at Fred.

Fred said, "I ran one of those stands for years. Just sitting there all day and half the night I couldn't help but get a few ideas for improving them. I made one so one man could set it up or take it down by himself if he had to move. What with the city changing regulations and imposing more and more

76

restrictions. And I made them more secure from break-ins."

"That's great." Buster said, his thoughts turning inward, "I'm a fireman and I had an idea for a tool once. But somebody beat me to it. Story of my life."

After a moment of silence, Helen said, "And don't they have buses in Bermuda?"

"Oh, yeah. They have six or seven bus lines. Take you all over the island. But then you're tied to their schedules. Suppose you're having a good time in some hotel or nightclub; they stop running at a certain hour. I just forget which. You don't want to be watching the clock if you're having a good time. If you have your own motor bike you come and go as you please."

"They have cabs, don't they?" Fred asked hopefully.

"Yeah. But it can be just like getting a cab in the rain in New York. The later it is, the fewer there are to respond."

"Does it rain much there? I mean this time of year."

"Not really. In the mornings there's a lot of rain clouds sitting off the island and you'd swear it was going to rain but it never does. Gets very dewy at night, though. Need a sweater or something at night."

Helen nodded at this as if making a mental note.

Buster, having brought his empty beer can up to body temperature, was debating whether or not to have another. He checked his watch again. It was 6:35. Thirty-five minutes to touch down, at least another ten before she got to the luggage carousel. That's forty-five minutes.

77

Fred and Helen were content to sit silently holding hands. Buster was married fourteen years. Or was it forty?

Buster said, "By the way, if you go to one of those limbo dances don't let them talk you into trying to limbo under one of those poles."

"Oh, we won't." Helen promised.

"That's what I said but after a couple of rum swizzles you think you can do anything. I tried it. Almost broke my back. Good thing I was anesthetized. Know what I mean? Had to spend the whole next day in the pool. Between the head and the back I was crippled for two days. What time's your flight?"

Fred consulted his boarding pass. "Seven-thirty. I wonder if we should get started."

"Naw," said Buster. "You got forty-five minutes at least. Why stand in line? What gate?"

"Seventeen."

"That is down the other end. So you sprint the last hundred yards."

Fred looked at Helen. They shrugged in unison.

Buster said, "And you have to climb Saint David's lighthouse; two hundred and some steps. Give you flat feet but the view is magnificent; see the whole island."

"No elevators?" asked Helen.

"No. And the coral. Pink coral. Makes the sand pink. Take a walk out on the coral and look down into the water. It's so clear you can see down twenty feet or more. You see these big fish gliding by. But wear flat shoes. Coral is slippery and sharp. Pick bananas right off the trees. What a place. They have pine trees and palm trees growing side by side."

Helen was looking at Buster nostalgically. Fred looked from the beer can to his watch.

Buster said, "Don't let anybody talk you out of riding the motor bikes. Once in a while an accident. They were probably drunk."

Helen said, "I have absolutely no sense of balance."

"So you double up with Fred. And those horse and buggies are so lame. It's like being in a wheelchair or something."

Fred consulted his watch and shifted his weight on the seat.

Buster went on, "Only bad thing about it not being summer is you miss out on the snorkeling. They have like a game preserve for fish. They swim right up to you. The colors. They're beautiful. And there's the glass bottomed boats."

Fred said, "What boats?"

"For a couple of bucks a guy takes you out in a motor boat with a glass bottom. He explains all the different kinds of fish. It's nice."

Helen said, "Oh, that sounds like fun. We have to try that, Fred."

"Don't forget your sun block. Behind the knees and the instep. Two very vulnerable places. You don't realize you're burned till it's too late."

Fred and Helen nodded politely.

"In Hamilton, where the cruise ships dock, everyone visits the Hog Penny Inn. Paneled in dark wood with English hunting prints. They have the dark English beer on tap. But watch the steps coming in out of the bright sunlight. Inside, you have to go down two steps, then across a room and up two steps to the bar. Everybody trips and they all laugh. It's all in good fun." Buster stood up. "I believe I'll have another. Can I get anyone anything?"

Fred said, "No, thanks."

Buster went into the passageway and called the company. Freddie a Probie answered the phone, "Engine Three-forty. You light'em. We fight'em."

"Freddie, some day that's going to come back and bite you in the ass. How do you know I'm not the Chief's wife?"

"What? This is the public phone. We can say what we want. We pay for it."

"Any word on Feeny?

"No. Costello is up there. He called in. The effin Fire Commissioner and all his ass kissers are there to get their pictures taken. They chased the fireman out of the room to make room for the photographers."

"How are the guys?"

"Okay. You know, they wouldn't say shit if they had a mouthful. Where are you, home?"

"No. J.F.K. Picking up the wife from Chicago. I'll call later."

"Ten-four."

Buster got on a short line and wrapped his hot palm around a frosty Bud. He rolled the can across his arid forehead as he moved towards the cashier. He was back at the table before he realized Fred and Helen were gone. His coat hung on the back of his chair. The table was cleared.

Buster was taken aback. Why had they left so abruptly? He walked quickly towards the sliding glass doors, upsetting a jutting tray on a table along the way. As he reached the doorway he spotted Fred and Helen walking rapidly away in the direction of the southern flights. Fred had on the overcoat he must have been sitting on at the table. The top of gray curly head came barely to Helen's padded shoulder. His shoulders swiveling, Fred threw out first one leg and then the other like an angry soccer forward kicking the imaginary ball out of the path of an

80

opponent, but without the springy recoil, each step planted before him with the finality of a hanging judge's gavel. His knees seemed hardly to bend as each leg in turn arched across the floor; his heavy torso swaying to stay balanced. As the soles of his shoes slapped the floor like the stropping of the barber's razor, he would lurch forward, then roll, then lurch and roll again. In his left hand Fred held a new three suiter bouncing along just above the terrazzo floor, his other hand holding tightly to Helen. Helen had a decided limp, bobbing up and down, and seemingly being jerked towards Fred with each step as their tandem march failed to achieve any rhythm. Buster had what he called a flash; Fred was a midget, no, a dwarf.

Buster stepped out of the restaurant and checked a monitor. The Bermuda plane wasn't due to leave for another forty minutes. Why had they taken off so abruptly he wondered? His recollections were fuzzy. Had he said anything off-color? He could see if he had had one too many but he wasn't drunk. Hell, he only had one beer here. Then, of course four or five with the guys, but that was hours ago. He looked at his watch. With difficulty he brought it into focus. It looked like 6:45. Buster looked up at the large arched window; what the hell was he doing here anyway? Oh, yeah, had to pick up the wife, Maureen. He sucked on the can in his hand, draining it. A Port Authority Policeman strolled over and motioned him back into Cuisine of the Clouds. He motioned to the cop; oh, no trouble pal, with a wave and a lopsided grin. Buster said to himself, I understand you have your hands full with these weirdoes that gravitate to airports.

Retrieving his coat, Buster decided against thinking, I'll have to take a fuckin' lecture as it is when that plane lands. He started for the Chicago arrivals gate, bumping into people along the way. He came to a phone and called the firehouse. Pauly answered.

"Feeney's dead. Steve just called from the hospital. He looked like a mummy, he said. His three-piece set was all burned away. I shouldn't say it, but it's better. This job sucks! Yeah, see you tomorrow."

Buster stood among the friends and relatives eagerly waiting for friends and relatives at the luggage carousel, each searching for a familiar face. When he saw Maureen, he rose up and down on his toes waving to her until she saw him. She smiled briefly, automatically, as to someone who has been sent to pick you up, no more. They had nothing to say to each other, watching the infinite variety of luggage spilling onto the stainless steel carousel and trundling round and round, that same pink vinyl suitcase with the white poodle coming into view like a broken record, again and again.

When Maureen had fished her bag out of the whirlpool and gotten close enough to smell Buster's breath, she said, "Christ! Give me the keys. I'll drive."

Years later, well after he had stopped drinking and Maureen had thrown him out, Buster realized how kind Fred and Helen had probably meant to be to him by hurrying away while he was getting that beer, saving him at least some embarrassment, jabbering along about limbos and lighthouses. Mourning alone with a beer can doesn't count. There's no community in that. As Maureen always said, he had no finer feelings.

ATTRIBUTION RESTORED

Simon Morrow, yes the Simon Morrow the literary critic had been in the business for forty years; for ten years out of college he wrote, 'his pen a white hot poker burning through the farce and foible of his time', or so proclaimed the jacket blurb of his first novel. His second novel's jacket was more modest and as Wilde would have said, 'had every reason to be'. Simon always referred to it as his second effort when in fact it was his last. So stung was he by the critics that he found his only refuge was in joining them. For thirty years now he had been a talk show gadfly, Sunday supplement reviewer and occasional guest lecturer, all honing his critical skills. Of course he knew all about publishing as second raters often do, but the fire had died down, banked for years, almost out several times, drowned in drink and self-pity. His criticisms were tart. He found little to praise, he held out hope for few.

As a young adjunct at a small college, Simon was assigned Writing 101. After a few years he came upon a promising student who even he couldn't miss, beauty and brains. They married. Shamelessly, he stole her best ideas. And as only the young, with their open ended view of life can do well, he told himself he would repay her, lift her up to that rarified plateau he would surely come to occupy, or some such claptrap. One day he came home from school and found her dead. Her heart, the doctor said. Didn't he know? She told the doctor she would tell him when the time was right, when he developed a spine. He imagined she had finally come to see him for the shallow fraud he was.

Fortunately for him, his first book came out soon after and the fanfare was a merciful distraction, helped along by the Dewar's he took in like a sponge. The second book was more of a publisher's hopeful investment; more payment deferred.

Reeling from his second effort, he became interested in his tormentors, more Stockholm etc., as practiced by those who crept onto the now quiet battlefield to pick over the corpses of effort. Writing is exploring. Most never find the riches of the literary Indies, lost up blind alleys of purple prose, Sargasso Seas of compromise and Department Chair's teas. Some years went by and as a lecturer he had learned to limit himself to one or two chardonnays at the end of the day to relax his face, to affix his donnish smile for the shrinking number of women who would brush a hair off his stained lapel. "Don't you think Pope is overrated?" No, your mind is under funded, he said to himself as he ground a cashew into paste.

And then ten years ago, he was at another small college, teaching "Introduction to Prose, Essays and Verse 101". He sat one day in his small office, going over essays, his penance. He had Mozart on the public station, a tether to sanity. One essay jumped up at him, "What Nadine Gordimer did for me." He set it aside. He went on to the next fumbling efforts. But it stayed with him like the scent of a pressed rose in an old book that falls open. In the morning he reread it. Good, very good. He looked at the name, Alice Whitcomb. He couldn't place her. For once, he looked forward to his next class. He took down an old collection of Gordimer's short stories and slipped them into his ratty briefcase.

At the next class he identified Alice, attractive, fresh farm girl. To his horror, Simon noticed she was holding hands under the desks with a second string something-or-other. Simon had written on her essay, "'A', try a short story."

After class Alice came up to him on the sidewalk and introduced herself and Buzz. "Buzz is a four-letter man." "Really, I find I need all twenty-six." She thanked him for the 'A'. Simon thanked her, he had many 'A's but few people to give them to. Buzz asked if he, too, should write a short story. Simon tried his old analogy. "You know, writing is like cooking. We've seen Maurice do the duck l'orange so effortlessly on TV while carrying on a scintillating conversation that we can't understand why our effort on the hotplate under the eaves doesn't taste the same."

Buzz thought duck was very greasy. Alice thanked Simon and led Buzz off to Starbucks.

At the next class, they turned in short stories. He packed them into his case and went to supper in the local diner down the road from the campus. You did not face reading short stories on an empty stomach, some done on ruled spiral notepaper. Simon eschewed his usual chardonnay, knowing he was ultra critical on even one ounce.

At home he set Alice's aside and flew through the other short stories. Surprisingly, Buzz's wasn't bad, a certain rugged, junior high simplicity. Then Simon picked up Alice's; please let it show merit. He read it a second time. He got up and had a small chardonnay. He stared out the window at the houses across the street, gabled roofs, chimneys, and TV antennas, a slice of lemon moon hung above. He sat down, holding the short story before him, "A Time Lent". Who did she remind him of? Not his wife. A little of Margaret Atwood, a little Ursula K. Le Guen, some Andrea Barrett, who? Still, a hint of Louis Auchencloss. Simon looked up at the shelves of books against the wall. This talent must be nurtured, if he never did another thing. It was no accident that this girl was in his class, sent to him. He was about to uncork the chardonnay, no; he realized he didn't need it. He had a quest. He slept like a baby.

After each class, Simon recommended a writer to Alice, Annie Proulx. If she had read Proulx, then Bobby Ann Mason, Auchencloss, Alice Munro. Buzz was always in tow.

Buzz, it turned out, was a senior and an English Major, (God help us!). Alice was a sophomore. He took the class only to be near Alice, how sweet. Graduation Day came. After the circus on the quad, Simon looked for Alice. Her roommate set him straight; Alice and Buzz had left in his Duster towing a U-Haul, bound for fame and fortune in New York. Back at his office, Simon found a thank you note from Alice for all he had done for her and Buzz. Buzz!? He slumped in his chair, if only he could have gotten her to fall in love with writing. Buzz. There is always a Buzz.

Let's fast-forward ten years to late last spring. Madison Avenue is closing shop for the day. Simon runs into Alice as she is leaving an office building. They were both flustered, "Come for a drink, dinner." She looked frazzled. "Oh, love to, but must run. Pick up the children at after-school and day-care, get home to Buzz. If I don't cook something, he doesn't eat. (Please test that theory.) Wonderful seeing you again." He thrust his card on her. "If you don't call me, I shall tell the police you stole my pencil box or something." He watched her disappear into the evening crowd.

The following week Simon and Alice had lunch. She praised his collection of criticisms. He pressed her about her writing.

"Oh, on hold, really. Writing copy for soap and perfume."

"No one can say your writing stinks."

"Buzz is struggling on his book."

"You can't abandon your writing. You'll come to despise yourself, your life. It's not a gift. It's a duty to examine the life around you and translate for the mass of fools who need spiritual direction, who need someone to tell them they are not irredeemable and absolute shit." Some people looked around. "I'm sorry." Simon lowered his voice.

The light came back on in her eyes; "I do have some jottings I could send you."

"Do."

Oh, of course Simon looked at the children's pictures and oohed and aahed. Tom and Julie, or something like that.

The next week he received a slim manila envelope at his office at the magazine. It was from Alice. He closed his door – his 'Do Not Disturb' sign.

Simon took a deep breath and opened the envelope. He read a short story. He read it again. He could feel his pressure rise. He loosened his tie. She still had it. She had the human condition by the throat. Characters ruled by emotion over reason, by custom over justice, all our foolish neighbors down pat.

Simon stared at the office door. All this talent hidden under a bushel named Buzz. Buzz buzzing around her head. Buzz, without the value of a fallen sparrow. He must do something. Simon mused, if he could just get his hands around Buzz's neck, he would gladly pay the piper.

At their next luncheon, Alice rambled on about Buzz's struggles. He had had one novel seven years earlier, since then three manuscripts rejected.

"Some of us have only one book in us. The sooner we realize that, the better for all."

"I sometimes feel I trapped him into marriage. If he were free..."

"That sounds like an excellent solution. Divorce him. Let me finish. Maybe you're holding each other back. Is it the money? I can place the story you sent me tomorrow. I'm sure you have more. I can see it in your eyes."

"Oh, I couldn't do that. He needs me."

"He needs his mommy or a swift kick."

"Please."

"Sorry. None of my business. But, my God, you have talent. Don't throw it away. It may not be there tomorrow. I know. It's like smoke. Constantly changing shape until finally it's gone."

"I must run."

When Simon didn't hear from Alice for two weeks he called her office, "Send me what you're working on or I'll call Buzz and tell him just what a monstrous injustice he's committing."

Three days later Simon received a thickish envelope, three short stories by Alice. He put them in his briefcase and left the office early for his place upstate.

Simon had a small cabin on a large lake in the Catskills. He enjoyed mowing the lawns and then floating in the lake in an old black truck tube under a large straw hat, sipping a large gin and tonic. His nearest neighbor was Zazzi, a total sensualist. She was not stupid but preferred bedding to reading, exercise without eyestrain. They remained no more than good friends. Zazzi would come over in a homemade bikini once made of petite doilies but now of large bandanas. She had men over to her house but never brought them to Simon's.

She sprawled in a tube and told Simon all about the men in her life until he erupted with laughter.

"Zazzi, if these poor guys could hear you, they would never get another erection again.

"Don't worry about me, darlink. I can raise the dead from between the barracks bags."

Simon told her all about the Affaire Alice.

"Send him to me, Simon. I will make him forget her."

And an idea was born.

Simon made himself Alice's agent and placed the three stories. He hoped the checks would raise her self-esteem.

When next they met, Alice was depressed.

"I thought you and Buzz would be pleased with the checks."

"Haven't told him yet. That's all we'd need, me bringing in money from writing."

Simon took a breath, "Look, I was thinking. Have Buzz send me his manuscript. I'll look it over."

"Oh, would you?"

"No promises. But only if you continue to work."

"Okay, and now I can afford to have someone look after the kids after school."

Several days later Simon received the dreaded manuscript from Buzz. He would need his inner tube and G.and T. to tackle this, he thought.

Back at the lake, Simon was appalled to realize Buzz's manuscript was no more than a plagiarism of several of Alice's short stories cobbled together. He hung his head. A breeze pushed him against the willow branches at the bank.

When next he and Alice lunched, Simon was beside himself. He threatened to expose Buzz, at least to himself. Alice said if he did, she would never pick up a pen again. She stormed out of the restaurant. Simon had palpitations.

The next day his doctor told him he had an irregular heartbeat. Simon consulted with Zazzi.

"Maybe he could work up here, alone. Without the wife and kiddies, without distractions, except for me, of course."

"Would that be cricket?"

"Cricket I don't play. Only indoor sports, darlink."

Simon called Buzz at home.

"Read you manuscript. Shows promise. Needs work, of course. I was wondering, sometimes a change of scenery. I have this place upstate, remote. I'll be away for two weeks. I understand Alice will have to stay in town, but now that you have someone to look after the children. Might do you some good. – Good. I'll email directions. My neighbor will have the key. Yes, just down the road. Zazzi. Just call her Zazzi. No, no, think nothing of it. All in the service of art."

Simon contrived to go to some seminar or other near Boston. After a week, Zazzi called on his cell phone, "Listen darlink, either your friend is dead below the belt or I'm losing it. I did everything but tie him up. I'm off the case. I'm booked into a spa in New Mexico, also a nip and a tuck. I'm due. Water my plants. See you in five or six weeks. Ciao, baby."
"Click!"

Simon said to himself, on to plan 'B'. He returned to the cabin. Empty, the area around Buzz's laptop was strewn with balls of discarded typing paper. From the window he saw Buzz sitting on the dock, his head bent.

Simon snapped on the computer, went to the weather, temperature at noon was 78 degrees, expected to fall to 68 degrees by 2:00 p.m., a typical summer storm, maybe a squall coming. It should hit around three. Hadn't he been drenched many a time out on the lake?

He thought of leaving a letter for Alice. No, too incriminating, too premeditated. His lawyer would contact her about the will. He had no relatives.

There would be little activity on the lake at this hour, with school still in session and none when the storm popped up. Simon had two rowboats; an aluminum one with floatation pockets under the seats, and the old green woody he favored a flat bottom you could stand up in without rocking the boat, to cast among the shadowy submerged rocks where the big guys hid.

Simon put on his large straw hat and picked up two rods. He put two ice cold six-packs in the cooler and strolled down to the dock, passing the tall poplars he planted years ago to give some shade to the cabin in summer, and the tight row of firs to break the wind in winter, past the mulch pile of kitchen scraps and grass cuttings which gave him the sweet smelling loam the following spring used for getting shrubs and saplings rooted in this shaley, clay soil, good only for grass for dairy cows.

When Simon stepped onto the dock, Buzz looked up with a start, "Simon!"

"Buzz, how's it going? I see you've been busy. I spoke early. Boring. Got away early. Hope I'm not disturbing you?"

"Hardly. Just taking a break. That neighbor of yours, Zuzzi." Buzz shook his shaggy head.

"Zazzi. I should have warned you. Lock your doors at night. Anyway, let's get out on the lake. It has magic powers. Clears the cobwebs."

"I'm in." Buzz stood up and stretched. "What can I do?"

"Grab that anchor and the oars out of the aluminum. The woody is bigger. Put the anchor in the bow. That's the front." Simon sat in the stern and slowly pulled out the starter cord. It was badly frayed. He let it rewind slowly to insure it was evenly wound. It should hold for one or two more pulls.

Buzz sat in the middle facing forward, Simon started the kicker and away they went, cutting a white trail across the placid lake. Simon rubbed his free hand along the well-worn gun'al. She rides nice, he thought.

Simon surveyed the lake, empty. He could just make out the leading edge of the storm clouds on the eastern horizon. It was hot and the breeze felt nice on their faces. Simon looked at the back of Buzz's head, empty of course.

"Have a beer, Buzz. Don't be shy."

"Cool. You?" Buzz popped a beer.

"Later."

They dropped the mushroom anchor among a submerged pile of glacial boulders about a football field's length off a small island covered in pines. A swim he could manage if it came to that. But he didn't think it would.

Simon said, "Why don't you sit in the bow, balance us off? Won't get our lines tangled."

Buzz turned around and sat in the small bow seat. The boat swung on its anchor, pushed by a slight breeze, a foreshadowing of the storm that would come up behind Buzz. They took up their poles. Simon bated Buzz's with a wiggly worm. The ripples from their casting faded away.

Simon said, "This is the best fishing hole on the lake. It's easier than going to the fish store. The fish congregate here because they feel safe among the rocks and shadows. They always will. They can't change. They don't reason. We've learned to take advantage of their fixed lifestyle. But they're superior to us in one thing. They don't need us."

A pair of ducks flew overhead. Buzz said, "They look like bowling pins with wings."

"That's good." but Simon felt he had heard the analogy before. He looked up, the sky still blue as a baby's eyes. The sun was in the west, the clouds in the east. The storm would be on them while the sun still shone. He had on file: none of Buzz's four letters was for swimming.

Buzz said, "Wonder why the water smells like corn stalks?"

"That's the vegetation falling into the lake and dissolving, pine needles, leaves, falling branches. Probably brought to the surface by a little methane gas."

"Corn sounds nicer."

"With just a hint of charcoal starter." Simon heard the distant rumble of thunder. He looked at Buzz, no reaction. Buzz had gone through the first six-pack. The blue water was now mixed with little patches of pewter gray, like curled floor tiles. The sky darkened behind Buzz's head. A cold gust of wind blew down the lake; whitecaps appearing like fresh linen pulled from dresser drawers.

Buzz turned around, "Whoa, where'd that come from?" he rubbed his hand across his mouth, gauging the distance to the island, glancing back across the wide expanse of water they had crossed, no longer placid. "Should we be thinking of getting back? You know, I can't swim. Great time to be bringing it up, I know."

Simon looked past Buzz's head, smiling, "summer storm. Full of sound and fury but they don't last long. We have two good hours yet. Time to get supper."

The boat tugged at the anchor and bobbed lightly. Buzz looked at the sky and at Simon.

Simon felt a slight skip in his chest, a warning, a summons? At his last check-up the doctor said a heart muscle was sluggish. And then, when they manage to drain the color from your face they say, "Oh, nothing to worry about."

Buzz kept watch on the sky.

Buzz, a blot on the escutcheon of literature. Simon saw it as his duty to give him his final 'F'. Simon knew that the unknown beyond was a condition void of time and choice, only an acute awareness, paved with lost opportunities to do good, to set a good example. You would be ever aware of the little you had done and all you had failed to do.

Simon knew somehow that what Buzz was doing to Alice was some kind of sin. And if he was right and did nothing to break the cycle wasn't he also committing sin? Didn't his years tell him what was being lost better than the young? Wasn't he under some obligation to act?

Their poles hung like pointers above the still water.

"So, how's the writing coming?"

Buzz shrugged, "It's like I have the nouns of one language and the verbs of another and can't match them up."

"Listen, Buzz. I don't want to interfere but you know I know something about this game. Some of us, myself included, only have one book in us."

Buzz shrugged. They sat angled away from each other.

Simon went on, "Maybe a radical change is called for. Maybe you and Alice need some time away from each other. A new perspective, maybe your relationship has gotten too symbiotic. We don't confront our problems as long as there's someone there to tell us they don't exist."

"You mean divorce?"

"Nothing so drastic. That would upset the children. No, call it a retreat, a hiatus. Besides, absence makes the heart grow weaker, er, fonder. I have a friend, runs a writers' colony in Colorado. Owes me a favor. Wouldn't cost anything. Fresh start. Get your bearings back. After all, with the income from her short stories …"

"Short stories? Income?"

"Didn't Alice tell you? I placed three of her stories."

"No, she didn't. Trying to spare me. Always the thoughtful angel."

"I have to tell you, that manuscript you sent me, well, obviously it was all lifted from Alice's work."

"How do you know she didn't steal from me?"

"Because you've turned three silk purses into one sow's ear. The short stories are all unrelated and you tried to count apples and oranges. It didn't compute."

Buzz leaned forward; "When you're hungry you steal. You don't know how many times I've tried to stop, to drop it all. I know two wrongs don't make a right and all that but stealing doesn't seem so bad if it can hold back despair, even for only a little while. I'd look at the garage mechanic when he was tracing an electrical fault in the car, the enthusiasm in his voice, his face, and his posture. My God, I wanted to jump right into his overalls. I know I should let it go. I know I suck. But I can't. I can't."

A sheet of rain was coming towards them like a cavalry charge. Simon watched the rain closing in, veiling the houses, the docks, the stately, gothic pines guarding the shore. The boat pulled furiously

95

on the anchor line like a lamb staked out for the approaching lion.

Buzz turned and saw the black wall of rain. He fumbled with the anchor line, "God, we better get out of here."

Simon said, "Don't pull up the anchor until I get the engine started or else we'll be swept into the middle of the lake."

The rain hit like lead from a shot tower. The water was up to their ankles. Simon turned and jerked at the outboard starter cord and it came away in his hand. Buzz's face twitched as he stared at the cord dangling from Simon's hand, "I said I'd call today. Another broken promise."

Simon stared hard at Buzz cringing like a shaking rat in the torrent and said to himself, oh, who am I? He reached under his seat and pulled out an orange life jacket.

"Here. Put this on."

Buzz quickly donned the jacket.

"What about you? Where's yours?"

"I don't need one. I can swim. It's only a short swim to the island."

The water was up to the seats. Between the full gas tank, the engine and the pull of the anchor, they were going down. The waves were diving into the boat. Buzz turned and twisted, squinted and stared.

"Oh, my God, what'll we do? What'll we do?"

"Save your breath. The boat won't sink. It's wood."

Simon unbolted the outboard and let it fall into the lake along with the red gas tank. It was like rearranging the proverbial deck chairs. The boat settled into the waves. Buzz clung to the gun'als.

"We'll slide into the water and turn it over. We'll hang on 'til it's over. Then right it."

96

Simon clutched his chest. He fell forward onto his knees. He looked up at Buzz and squeezed out a short laugh.

Simon opened his eyes. He was staring up at the blue sky washed clean by the storm. Faces appeared over him, saying, "He's coming around." "You can't kill these old guys."

Simon said, "What...?"

The EMTs hustled him into an ambulance and they sped off. Simon felt a bulk around himself. It was a life jacket, his orange life jacket.

It was a long winter.

Summer sunlight flooded Simon's wide sun porch overlooking the lawn, the dock and the float out on the lake. Small sailboats slid by, their sails like white handkerchiefs in blue breast pockets. Alice sat before the computer, typing away. Every once in a while she would rotate her neck, look out and see Simon sprawled in a deck chair and little Tom and Julie frolicking in the shallows of the beach. She smiled and got back to work.

Simon finished a dog-eared manuscript and stared at the title page. "'<u>FALLEN ANGELS</u>' by Buzz Graham." He dropped it unceremoniously next to his chair, "Utter tripe." He looked up at the squabbling noises coming from the children.

"Stop fighting. Start swimming. Race out to the float and back."

Julie whined, "Oh, what's the use. Tom always wins."

Tom said, "That's 'cause I'm a better swimmer."

"No it's not. It's only because you're bigger. But you may not always be. Now get in there and swim. Remember, you only lose if you quit."

They turned and dove into the lake and raced for the float.

Alice stood at the printer watching it spit out pages.

Simon sat back, clutching his cane and said softly, "You're only beaten if you quit."

Alice appeared at his side, "Ready for some lunch?"

Simon looked up; "I'll get it. You keep working."

"It's all ready. Come on, you two, lunch!"

She sat on the edge of the small wicker table; "It's all bubbling to the surface just as you said it would. I've almost finished the chapter. I'll have it for you after supper."

Simon looked at her smiling face, her hair in a ponytail, just like Julie's, "Put it away until Monday. Let it jell."

"Oh, you always say that. I can't wait for you to read it."

"Remember, a first draft is no more than a blueprint."

"I know. All good writing is rewriting."

"Clichés are none the less true."

Alice stood. She looked out over the lake, "How calm it can be. How deceiving. At least they'll always have the memory of their father as a hero."

"Yes. Shouldn't have happened like that."

"Thank God you're here to teach them how to swim. Heaven knows they'd never learn from Buzz. He was desperately afraid of the water. What is it, 'Man proposes; God disposes?'"

Simon looked up at her, "Yes." He clutched his cane and made to rise.

Alice said, "Stay. I have it all made. I'm bringing it out."

She walked back to the house. Simon waved the children in off the float where they were sitting conspiratorially in the sun, becoming 'them' against 'us'.

Simon looked out over the lake and up at the sky, saying softly, "My God, what the fuck have you done?"

"Oh, no, Simon; I says when it's quitin' time."

Rafting on the Imjin

The truce signed, the war was over. Up to that point, at least three times that I know of, I was almost killed: that sniper's bullet that buried itself in the trench wall an inch above my head, sand trickling from the pencil sized hole down my neck; the probing mortar rounds 'walking' down the outpost trail, searching for our patrol as we hugged the earth in fear and prayer, released from gravity with each impact, -suddenly stopped, when tradition said they should have walked right through us to the foot of the hill; that round that burned right through the 'S' of USMC on Mahoney's dungaree jacket, that last night we traded watches. At nineteen I was indestructible.

Anderson, Lopez and I trudge down to the Imjin for a swim. Sunning myself on my smoothed out dungarees, my fingers toy absently with something rusty, conical in the shaley sand. I sit up ramrod straight, afraid to look at my hand. Ritchie and Jesùs glide by on their air mats, behinds wet and pale, laughing, splashing, the silty brown, mother-of-pearly river roller coasting by. Finally, I have to look down at the rusty metal object I have been unearthing. It is an unexploded shell, nose up, a one-five-five or something off the Missouri, landed in the muddy, swollen Imjin of 1950 or '51 when I was in English 2 or Biology 1. Is the rusting process of the springs and plunger mechanism now almost complete? Was my plopping my ass down on the riverbank the last concussion but one that it could take? I stare straight across the river at the summer green rice paddies and the blue, blue sky. How much more cruelly an unexploded shell kills, again and again over many years. I sit there, so still, growing old and afraid.

Putting Something Aside

Saturday morning again at the Ryan home in Flatbush as Dick Ryan storms around the kitchen in his loafers, chinos and sweatshirt, absently brushing his grey crew-cut with one hand while delivering his usual Saturday morning tirade against some failing of the republic or of his twelve year old son, Ritchie. Bending over his plate, mopping up his egg yolk with a slice of bread, Ritchie is maddeningly averting his head from his father's wagging finger. Ritchie learned years ago when he was eight, not to pay too much attention to dad, in general, and especially on Saturday mornings when he was hung over from Friday night's beer from his club. Ritchie is a C+ student and his ambitions gravitate towards the sea. On his way home from school on Thursday, the warm breeze had been blowing from the south and he could smell the sea, clean and new.

May, in her pink robe and rollers, is applying butter to her toast as though it were caviar, deciding whether to go shopping at Kings Plaza or the Staten Island Mall. It's her turn to choose. It has turned out to be such a nice day that she is glad she gave her hair a good rinse last night. She'll be damned if she'll let her sister, two years older, see a grey hair. Maybe she'll take Joanne to that restaurant on the south shore next to the body building gym.

It's these warm, leisurely family breakfasts on Saturdays that make them all subconsciously yearn for Monday.

"What the hell's the matter with this kid, May?" dad was saying, "When is he going to learn to make an intelligent decision? When the hell is he going to start to grow up?"

May said, smiling at her only son, Ritchie, "Here, dear. Finish this bacon. I'm full."

"Thanks mom."

May said to Dick, "Now don't start blaming Ritchie for doing exactly what you're always telling him to do!"

Dick held his hands out as if he was holding a tray, "But this one had a uniform on."

"No matter." snapped May, "You're always telling him not to let anyone in the house when we're not home. Well, that's what he did."

Dick shook his head at his wife as if she was a dull child, "But it was obvious that this one worked for the gas company. He had a uniform on, didn't he? Otherwise, let's face it, May; nobody would ever open their door today. Not with what they're hiring these days." he rubbed his closed eye lids to give his bloodshot eyes a break from the bright sun.

Ritchie said, "You said never let any..."

"Don't start telling me what I said. You've got to start making intelligent decisions. You're not a baby anymore, Ritchie. Grow up, will you?"

May said, "Dick, didn't you say you were meeting the guys at the club at eleven?"

"Yeah."

'It's eleven-fifteen now."

Dick shouted, "You be home by five, Ritchie." as he started for the front door.

Ritchie's head bobbed up from his plate, "By five?"

May made a face at her husband.

Dick said, "Well, you be home by dark, anyway." May and Dick both remembering that ever since Ritchie was old enough to take care of himself, May had taken to going shopping with her sister on Saturdays and eating out. Dick had taken to going over to his store front club to relive his misspent youth, playing pool and drinking beer. Then he would come in and flop on the sofa until May came in three or four martinis to the good and chased him up to bed. Ritchie had never given them any trouble, so things had just drifted along this way. Dick's ordering Ritchie to be home by dark was really Dick's father speaking to him, twenty five years ago. Ritchie was always home by dark. He liked to cook, after a fashion. May always made sure there was something easy to heat up in the refrigerator.

After Dick had left for his club, May said, "You know, Ritchie. You could have let the meter reader in, yesterday. Now we'll get an estimated bill and they're always higher."

Ritchie said, "Dad makes the rules. They're his rules, not mine." arching his thin eyebrows in his infuriatingly pious manner.

May wanted to shake him, "Well," she smiled, "where are you off to today, dear?"

"Me and Barney are going down by the marina, crabbing."

"Who's Barney?" May said, examining all ten nails.

"Oh, he's a guy from school." he said, studying the wall clock.

May glanced at him briefly; "I don't recall you mentioning him before. Where does he live?"

"Somewhere on Nostrand Avenue. He just transferred to our school. He's a nice guy. He knows all about the ocean. He's going to be a marine biologist. Maybe I will be, too."

"That's nice, dear. Now don't fall in. Even though the weather is nice, remember the water is still too cold for swimming."

"Oh mom, stop worrying; will you?" Ritchie said as he slapped on his Mets cap and headed for the door.

"Don't forget your sandwiches."

As prearranged, Ritchie waited on Flatbush Avenue for Barney's bus. He only had to let one go by before Barney appeared, waving to him from the back window of the Green Bus. As the bus sped them on their way to adventure, they huddled in the back seat and giggled about who had goofed yesterday in school. They both had their lunch in brown sacks. Barney had his new collapsible crab trap from Sears that daddy had bought him two weeks ago after McDonald's, while he was getting new whitewalls put on his car. Ritchie had his crab net that his uncle Jimmy had given him.

Once they had passed Kings Plaza, the horizon flattened out and they could faintly smell the salt air through the open bus windows. Exhaust fumes dominated but were giving way. Speeding along between the golf course and the waterfront homes on Mill Basin Inlet, they were escaping into a fleeting adventure land that is not found much after one is twelve years old.

At the marina, they were the only ones to get off the bus. It was the rare person who had a boat and no car to take him to it. Not many people came to the marina to fish or crab because it was not allowed. Yet, Ritchie knew the shadowy water under the pilings and catwalks were a crabber's paradise. Mike, the owner let Ritchie onto the docks because his uncle Jimmy kept his cabin cruiser at the marina.

It was a sunny day, in late spring whose cool nights still kept the sand flea, fly and mosquito population down. A warm southerly breeze drifted across the Rockaway Inlet, nudging wavelets towards the crescent shore of Dead Horse Cove where the marina nestled. Whipped cream clouds gave definition to the blue sky. They strolled towards the main gangway that led down to the marine gas pumps and the long docks that stretched away from the beached barge that served as the office and Mike's home. Rows and rows of slips and bleached catwalks stuck out from the main docks like piano keys. More than half of the boats were out fishing and sailing. Like impatient riding crops whisking against twill, main halyards slapped against gently rocking aluminum masts, metal clips pinging against metal, the forest of masts caroling as an impudent speed boat's wake slapped their hulls. Ritchie and Barney hung over the railing, examining low tide; exposing dark green, mossy poles that held the docks in place, canted here and there like tarred gondola poles, festooned with glistening white barnacles. The dull grey-brown mud banks were alive with shiny fiddler crabs darting in and out of their holes. The sea's coverlet had rolled back to reveal half buried, old tires, beer cans and bottles; relics of a century hung up on waste.

They each bought cold sodas from the machine and watched men and women in faded and paint splattered jeans, removing paint cans and brushes from car trunks. They wore new baseball caps and white sun hats for the new season, chatted gaily and waved to other sailors. Many wore expensive watches and bracelets, not really old salts. They were coming down too late in the season to be starting to fix up boats.

Ritchie ran ahead, down the swaying, old gangplank, shouting over his shoulder at Barney that there was someone he wanted him to meet. Barney lagged behind, looking over these new surroundings. He hadn't seen one black person.

Ritchie ran up to an old tub of a thirty-footer, a creaking, listing old weather beaten Wheeler cabin cruiser, tied up to a partially submerged slip. Across the transom, in faded letters, was the name NORGE. Speedy Olsen, the captain of this once proud vessel, stood on the fantail in dirty old, grey, long john top and frayed and faded blue bell bottoms. He was scratching himself between the shoulder blades with an empty, long necked beer bottle. A scraggly mop of salt and pepper hair hung down over his furrowed and burnt brow into bushy yellowed eye brows. His teeth, noticeable by their absences, were like defaced, vandalized tombstones. His eyes were red, white and blue.

Ritchie's face, new minted from the treasury of good intentions, was shining as it never was at home. He had met Speedy for the first time at the close of the previous summer and renewed the friendship this spring. On Saturdays Speedy regaled Ritchie with stories of rum running in the Twenties: small, high-powered speed boats, outrunning deep draft Coast Guard Cutters, between and across the hundreds of uncharted, fog shrouded shallows and hassocks in the bays and inlets of the south shore of Long Island; of ship's carpenters working all through the night at removing machine gun bullets from wet hulls, and repainting and drying them under sun lamps before the Coastguardsmen came around in the morning looking for shot-up boats. Ritchie hung on every salty word that Speedy uttered. In Ritchie's dreams, Speedy and Long John Silver would merge.

Speedy was an old recluse and lived on board all year long. In winter he covered the boat with a large tarp which was now rolled back over the cabin. In one corner of the stern stood an avocado plant in an old butter tub, its young leaves reaching for the new sun. Speedy doubled as an unofficial night watchman. Mike didn't charge him rent and gave him free electricity to keep his bilge pump going.

Ritchie, knowing the custom, waited on the dock to be invited aboard. Speedy noted the altitude of the sun and then eyed this young Viking with a crab net.

Speedy, looked down at Ritchie, his grin spreading a network of creases through his weathered face, his voice rolling and creaking like an old wooden deck, "Wal. Ah think it must be Saturday if ah see your face around the dock. Come on aboard, Ritchie."

Ritchie laid his gear on the catwalk and clambered over the gun'all. Standing on the gently rocking deck, Ritchie felt that all the ports to adventure were open to him.

"Boy!" he exclaimed, "I bet you could sail anywhere in the world in a boat like this."

"Ah sure," Speedy nodded. Then he cocked an ear towards the hatch behind him. He had heard the electrical bilge pump stutter and hesitate, umbilical cord that kept the NORGE with its rotting planks, afloat. "Ah've joost got to check that damn pump. Be back." disappearing into the shadowy recesses of the cabin.

Barney had stopped a little way off and was watching. When Ritchie saw Barney, he waved him over to the boat, smiling.

Ritchie said, "Hey, Barney. Ain't this neat?"

"It's o.k."

"Man! I think it's cool. Come on aboard. See how it feels."

"Naw, come on. We came down here to go crabbing, didn't we? So, let's go crabbing, eh?"

Ritchie pestered him, "Come on for a minute. Don't be a chicken. See how it feels on deck. Come on."

Barney knew better than to go on someone's property uninvited, but..., "Whose chicken?"

Barney put one toe on the rub rail for purchase and vaulted easily over the gun'all, silently onto the deck.

The thrill of being 'aboard' seeped into the boys. They grinned wide-eyed at each other. There is something about having a deck under your feet that makes you feel free and important, and purposeful.

"Hey." Ritchie whispered, "Wouldn't it be cool to go looking for buried treasure in a boat like this?"

"Yeah, man. That would be neat."

Speedy came up on deck, clutching a warm, foaming bottle of beer in one hand, muttering, "Got to cut a new gasket for that damn pump.", and wiping his face with an old dirty towel. He stopped short when he saw Barney.

"Hey, you," Speedy growled, "What the hell you think you doing?"

Barney backed against the gun'all. Speedy seemed to have forgotten that Ritchie was there.

Ritchie said, "Eh, Speedy. It's okay. He's with me. Okay?"

Ritchie's face flushed, realizing he was apologizing for Barney. A quick glance at Barney's stone face showed him his defense had been received as an excuse rather than as testimony. And another crack appeared in the new foundation built from old plans.

Speedy dropped the towel and clenched a fist at Barney, "There be no niggers aboard my boat!"

As deftly as he had come, Barney vaulted over the side, landing lightly and whirling to face Speedy with chin proudly thrust forward, glaring back up at the greasy old honky. With a lump growing in his throat, Barney said to himself, 'Don't you cry, you mother. Just don't you cry.'

Ritchie pressed himself against the opposite gun'all. He could see only Speedy's broad back, with his one fist raised in the air. Ritchie was ashamed to be glad that he couldn't see Barney's face. More to the point; that Barney couldn't see his. He looked about the marina for someone to break it up, as happened when two boys would be fighting in the school yard. He searched the suddenly empty catwalks. The few people he could see seemed not to hear Speedy's shouting and cursing. They looked away and bent to their painting and cleaning. There would be no cavalry charging to the rescue with flags fluttering and bugles blaring, not ever again.

"Don't stand there glaring at me, you black bastard!" Speedy thundered down at Barney, taking an unsteady step towards the gun'all, "Get off this dock before I break your head!"

Clutching the rail behind him, Ritchie wished, 'Oh, God, why can't Barney be white?', and immediately he was convulsed anew with shame as, in lightening flashbacks, he recalled the time the Fitzpatrick brothers were beating him up in the empty school yard after school. The one that had him around the neck went sprawling one way, another tumbled another way and the third was getting up and running. Then they were all in flight. Barney was helping Ritchie up off the dirty yard. They were alone. Ritchie hadn't minded Barney's being black then; or when Barney had slipped him an answer on the math quiz. Ritchie's face burned from within. He knew these were not the reasons intended in guiding one in practicing the Golden Rule, love thy neighbor as thyself; but making decisions based on abstract principles was new to him.

Barney and Ritchie looked everywhere but at each other's eyes. Barney picked up his crab trap and lunch sack, glad of an excuse to turn away from his tormentor. He walked away as fast as he could, blindly, towards the end of the dock, screeching gulls mocking him from overhead. Ritchie sensed that that crucial time span may have expired wherein any lasting merit of a cowardly delayed act's commission is lost. Still, he must try. Standing up straight, Ritchie's eyes were moist as he brushed passed Speedy, towards the rail.

Speedy said, "You can stay, Ritchie. But ah don't allow no coons on my boat. They rob you blind. 'Sides, they be bad luck."

"He's my friend!" Ritchie said over his shoulder, his voice cracking. "We go to school together. You didn't have to say those things. You didn't have to be so mean. You're just the same as everybody else." Speedy made to put his arm around Ritchie's shoulder but Ritchie shook it off.

"He ain't your friend, Ritchie." Speedy shook a gnarled finger at him. "You watch'em. Give'em an inch and they take a mile. You see. In time, you see." he swayed against the rail.

Ritchie jumped over the side, grabbing up his net and lunch. He began running down the docks until he was out of earshot of Speedy's cackling voice, calling after him.

After looking around the slips awhile, Ritchie spied Barney at the end of the furthest dock where an old sand barge had been sunk as a breakwater for the marina. Ritchie hesitated.

Barney had busied himself and laid his trap. He was squatting at the edge of the dock, staring down at his fragmented reflection in the salty, rainbow oily water. How many times had he been told, he reflected, 'Stay with your own kind!' Then, he'd say, 'No! It shouldn't be this way.' Naw, he sighed, it

110

happened all the time, every day. And it would go on happening every day, just as regularly as the good things in life, like breathing and eating, and standing in the sun. He used to look up at his brothers and say, 'It'll be different. You'll see. People change. There's this guy I go to school with, Ritchie. He's o.k.!

Ritchie, standing alone in the long shadows cast by the sailboat masts, considered going home and pretending that the whole incident had never happened. It wasn't his fault that people were of different colors. Why did his day have to be spoiled? Why did he have to be made unhappy? Why did he feel guilty?

Ritchie came up behind Barney and their images merged in the oily green water. For awhile they listened to the halyard hooks tapping against the masts and the gulls squealing and turning above the returning fishing boats.

Barney said to the face in the water, "Why ain't you over with your honky friend?"

Ritchie shrugged, "I think he's drunk. He's usually a pretty nice guy."

Barney squinted up at his classmate, "Now, you don't really believe that shit, do you?"

Frowning, Ritchie squatted next to Barney. They were looking at each other's reflection in the water.

Finally, Ritchie, with forced good humor said, "Let's pull up the trap and see if we got anything."

Barney shook his head, "Just let it down. Too soon."

"Oh, all right."

His composure returning, Barney turned to Ritchie and said, "Why, Ritchie? Why?"

Looking at the horizon, Ritchie heaved a sigh, "I don't know. My uncle who owns the boat, he says people who act like that are scared of something. They have to make up reasons to think they're better than someone else."

Barney shook his head, "What do they have to be scared of? They have everything already."

"I don't know. Maybe some people are too afraid of running out of something, to share it with other people. They're just born cheap or scared inside, even before they know what money and things are."

Barney said, "Wish I had the money to buy this dock."

"Yeah. Me too."

They continued to talk of crabbing and fishing, of the sea and boats, but it was not the same between them as it was before Speedy. They ate their sandwiches listlessly and washed them down with sodas Ritchie got from the machine while Barney watched the trap.

Along about three o'clock, as the sun was bending towards the west, Ritchie said, "My folks won't be home for supper tonight. So I don't have to be home so early tonight."

Barney said, "So?"

Ritchie warmed to his topic, "Want to go for a pizza?"

Barney was thoughtfully silent.

Ritchie said, "I know a great pizza parlor on Avenue 'U'."

Barney made a face, "Naw. I can't. My dad is coming by here to pick me up. Every other Saturday, he picks me up and takes me out to eat someplace. Usually it's McDonald's."

Ritchie said, "Oh. Doesn't he live with you?"

"No. My mother and father don't get along. They're separated."

Ritchie said, "Hey, let's pull it up and see what we got."

"Yeah. Let's see."

Together they slowly hauled up the trap, grown heavy. There were eight large crabs and two babies in the sea weed draped trap

Ritchie said, "Boy! If only we had a pot, we could cook'em over on the beach."

"Yeah! There's plenty of drift wood on the beach, too."

"And fresh water from the barge... Oh, I forgot. You have to go with your father."

"Ah, yeah. And I better be getting up to the parking lot, too. Daddy gets mad if he has to wait."

Ritchie said, "What about the crabs?"

"You can have my share. Dad wouldn't let me take them in his car, anyway. Says they smell up the car. He's always spraying perfumy stuff in the car. Yuk!"

"Okay, I'll take'em home and put them in the freezer."

"Ritchie, do me a favor? Take my crab trap home with you. I'll get it during the week at school. OK?"

"Sure. I'll take care of it. I think I'll ask Mike if he'll lend me a big pot. I'll cook the crabs right on the beach, by myself." Ritchie shrugged, "See how they come out."

Barney said, "You mean; stay on the beach by yourself? It'll be getting dark by the time you get the water boiling, if I know you."

"Yeah. Why not? I can get a pizza anytime."

Barney reflected with a grin, "It would be cool." He gazed over at the quiet curve of the beach below the parking lot.

Picking up their gear, they began walking back over the networks of docks. The sun, bouncing off the water, danced on the smooth hulls, mostly white, and up into their down turned faces. The few shadows appeared black by contrast. They walked by yachtsmen in director chairs, under canopies strung over their booms, sipping scotch on the rocks, laughing lightly. Fishermen stood at their sterns, cleaning their catch and hoisting glistening cans of ice cold beer, their faces red-brown from the sun. Gulls whirled overhead, screeching to each other impatiently, waiting for the innards of the fish to be cast into the sea for them, for what other purpose could these silly creatures below them have? The wind had shifted and began to slacken off. The tall sailboat masts cast a forest of slender shadows across the slips and catwalks, like reaching fingers pointing at the small white beach next to the marina office. The parking lot was beginning to empty out. People were going home or out to dinner and maybe on further into the night, searching for what they had failed to find in the sea.

Climbing the gangplank to the barge, Barney said, "You ain't really going to stay on the beach and cook them crabs all by yourself, are you?"

"Sure. Maybe I'll give a couple to Mike if he gives me some salt. And the buses run late on the weekends.

Frowning, Barney said, "You ever cook crabs before?"

"No. But who can't boil water?"

"There's more to cooking crabs right than boiling water."

Ritchie shrugged, "When they're red, they're done."

Barney said, "I'd better take a look down the end of the lot. My father may be waiting. So. see you."

"Yeah. See you Monday."

Barney's father was leaning against the fender of his old white Caddy. He was wearing a blue suit with a white silk shirt, open down the front, and a thin gold chain around his neck. He was staring past his folded arms at his new shoes. Barney could see he was dressed for more than McDonald's; probably had a date later.

He trotted the last ten yards, "Hey! Daddy."

His father turned towards him and became animated, "Hey, Barney, my man, what's happening?"

The soul brothers shook hands and horsed around the lot, boxing and grappling. His father still thought of Barney as about eight years old. But Barney was old enough to hide his own embarrassment for his father's sake, at daddy's foolishness. Barney was glad Ritchie was just out of sight around the corner of the barge.

Barney's father was trotting around the front of the car, "Hey, Barney. We better get going if we're going to beat the crowd. Come on, get in."

Barney said, "Where we going, McDonald's?"

"Not today, my man. We're going to Lundy's in Sheepshead Bay for lobster."

"Lundy's! Lobster! Oh, boy!"

"Got me an O.T. check this week" his father said, getting behind the wheel and starting the engine. "Come on. We're late."

Barney stuck his head in through the open window on his side, "Daddy. I was crabbing today with this friend of mine from school..."

"Catch anything? Hey, get in."

"Daddy, his folks ain't home on Saturday nights. Can we take him with us?"

Daddy sighed, "Do we have to? I figured we'd be alone. Talk over old times. Just you and me. Dig?

115

You know, we don't get together that often. Boy, you're shooting up. Can't talk with strangers hanging on, can we?"

Barney looked over his shoulder. He saw Ritchie and Mike talking at the corner of the barge. He pointed at them and said, "Hey, daddy. That's him, Ritchie, talking to Mike. Mike runs the marina."

Daddy stiffened, "What, that white kid?"

"Yeah, but he's o.k. He ain't no red neck."

"Man, shit!" daddy turned off the engine, slapping his hand against the dashboard, "How many times I gotta tell you, Barney. Don't mess around with them honkys."

"But daddy, he ain't like the rest of..."

"No? Bullshit. They are all alike. I can see you're going to have to learn that the hard way."

"Then, he can't come?"

Daddy heaved another sigh, "Look, Barney. I ain't got nothing against this kid, here. Understand? But it's hard enough that I gotta work with them all week long. And I'll be damned if I'm going to socialize with them on my own time."

"You mean, you're prejudice just like you're always saying they are."

"Oh, grow up, Barney. Everybody's prejudice'. The whole world is prejudice'. I didn't invent it! So don't start getting so Christian with me all of a sudden. Nothing worse than a liberal soul brother."

"I'm sorry."

"You gettin' in?"

"I'm not hungry." Barney was pushing the sand around with his sneaker.

"Me neither, now." his father was staring out to sea.

"Is it o.k. if I stay here for awhile and take the bus home?"

116

"Barney, listen." his father turned towards him, "You're right to make friends with all kinds of people. I just don't want you to get hurt, that's all. Don't listen to everything I say. I'm a crank sometimes."

"I know, daddy. It'll be o.k. You'll see."

"But don't believe everything you hear, either. Dig?"

"I dig."

Daddy pulled out his wallet and extracted a fiver, "What you plannin' to do, cook you some crabs?"

"Yeah. How'd you know?"

"I used to go crabbin'. We'd bring our own pot and salt."

"Ritchie's getting a pot from Mike. Why don't you stay? We only got eight crabs but we could catch more easy, heh?"

"Naw. Got to meet some people downtown. Late now. Here. Get some sodas and what all."

Barney pocketed the fiver, "Thanks, daddy."

In Barney's face he saw his wife before she got hard, "Too big to give your daddy a kiss?"

Barney opened the door, bent in and gave his father a kiss and a hug like when he was a kid years ago.

Daddy said, "I'll call you during the week. That new school o.k.?"

"Yeah, it's o.k." Barney scrambled out and closed the door.

His father slipped the car into 'Drive, "You be good, hear?" he smiled.

"You be good. Don't speed." Barney waved.

Leaving the parking lot, daddy began to dig-out, but checked himself and eased into the evening flow of traffic heading for the Shore Parkway.

The sun was resting above the Jersey Highlands now as Barney came up behind Ritchie trying to start

117

a fire with damp cattails. He had the crabs in a large pot of water, sitting on some rocks.

"Man, shit!" said Barney, "You don't know nothing about crabs. Take'em out of the water. You don't put them in the water till it's boiling hard. We need dry paper and good wood."

"You going to stay?" Ritchie beamed.

"Yeah, I guess so." Barney tried to frown but it didn't come off.

"What happened to your father?"

"He was in a big hurry. He just dropped by to say, 'Hello', and give me this." displaying the five dollar bill.

"Wow! Five bucks."

Barney was all business now, "Look, you go get us some sodas and I'll get some dry wood for the fire."

Smiling, Ritchie took the fiver and started trudging through the sand to the barge. Barney shouted after him, "Get some old newspapers, too, if you can."

Barney looked at the setting sun, streaked with purple, and then down at the pot. He said to himself, Boy, are we going to have fun!

And what passed for their parents as another dull day in this rat race would become for Barney and Ritchie, although they didn't know it yet, an important day in the plus column of their lives. They had put something aside towards those days ahead when the sun wouldn't shine.

Rings and Recollections

Helen Fox had just laid four of her dead husband Fred's suits across his swivel chair when her daughter Marion rang the front doorbell. Marion is always prompt. She is here to lead her mother through the final stage of what she calls, 'closure'. Fred has been gone for six months. One must move on says Marion. But just where, thinks Helen? Already she has gotten her mother new return address stickers which say, 'Mrs. Helen Fox'. Helen was not ready for the 'Ms.' yet. But Helen is determined to use the 'Mr.& Mrs. Fred Fox' stickers until they run out. Today they will finally empty out Fred's old roll-top desk from which he had kept the books for his hardware store for the past forty-nine years of their marriage.

After filling one trash barrel full of yellowed receipts and bills, old calendars, seed catalogs and bygone promotional material, Helen sat back in Fred's swivel chair, rotating her wedding and engagement rings, remembering.

"You know, when your father was reported missing near the end of the war, he was somewhere in Germany. I went into a tailspin and my father had to put me into a nursing home for a while. I refused to eat. Couldn't sleep. I was very high strung. Then the telegram came saying he was OK and on his way home. Oh, I was very immature, easily rattled."

"Mom, some people call it 'love'."

"Oh, Fred's mother looked at me sideways, I can tell you. Can't blame her. We became real friends as time went on."

Marion shifted her perch on a foot-stool. She had heard these stories many times before, different versions from different people at different times, "Hard to believe, the way you raised us five kids. We always thought of you as the strong one."

"We weren't even officially engaged when he went into the army but we had what they used to call an 'understanding'"

"Oh, right. Better have it on paper today."

"The day your father asked me to marry him we took a stroll across the dam, watching the water plunge over the edge and down into the river below. He had been home a week or so and was easing back into the hardware store which his father ran then. We were both nervous. It was a beautiful day. July. I had on this enormous straw hat."

"Daddy said it rained."

"Rained? No, that must have been some other day. You know what a memory your father had. Like a sieve. Always got my birthday mixed up with our anniversary. Well, anyway, we sat down on a bench. Just like a bench in a park but with no trees. I was as nervous as a cat. He was mumbling how with his mustering out pay, he'd have just enough for a ring and a new car. I was really only half listening. Fred bought Cracker Jacks and we sat looking down at the falls and the river. Then out of the blue he jumped up and said he remembered an appointment he had made with a salesman at the store. His father still ran the store but I guess he was easing Fred into the responsibilities. I thought, my God, he's getting cold feet! I didn't know whether to laugh or cry. But that night he proposed at my house. Mom and dad threw a small party out in the back yard. Popped the question we used to say."

"And you lived happily ever after. How romantic. Now the engagement party is usually held in the lawyer's office while they draw up the prenupt agreement.

"But let me tell you, Marion. Your father gave me whatever strength I've acquired over the years, even if he was absentminded and didn't know north from south. Well, let's get on with the rest of this."

"Mom, look at this. It's the receipt from Newman's Jewelry Store for your engagement ring."

"A girlfriend of mine had seen Fred going into Newman's a couple of days before. Of course back then you pretended not to know so you could act surprised."

"The date on this is, July 18th, 1945."

"July 18th? That's the day we became engaged. A Saturday night. Then he must have only bought it that day."

"Hey, mom. Here's another old receipt. Also for an engagement ring at Newman's but dated July 15th, 1945. Three days earlier."

"Let me see them. Hmm, the earlier one is for a smaller stone than the one I have. That's not mine."

Marion said, "Daddy must have changed his mind about the size of the ring while you were out walking and rushed off to Newman's to exchange it before they closed. It was Saturday. Newman's always closes at one on Saturdays."

"I remember he became quiet and a little pale at one point, staring into the falls for several long minutes. But a lot of the veterans did things like that then."

"But if daddy exchanged the ring of the 15th for your ring why would he still have the receipt for the earlier one? Wouldn't Newman's take the receipt back when he bought the second ring?"

"Oh, I don't know, Marion. It's all so long ago."

"I guess you're right, all water under the bridge."

Mrs. Fox sat bolt upright, "Wait. The prize in the Cracker Jacks was a ring. I flung it into the falls. I was so nervous. I remember saying, 'Look at this piece of junk. It wouldn't interest a five-year old.'"

"And that's probably when daddy went pale and silent. My God, mom! You threw the first engagement ring away. That's why he had to run off to Newman's for another ring. He knew grandma and grandpa had the engagement party all set up for that night."

Her eyes glazing over, Helen said, "And knowing what a nervous Nelly I was, your father wouldn't tell me what I had done. Probably thought I'd jump into the falls after the ring. And that's <u>also</u> why he never <u>did</u> get that new car he always wanted. In fact, every car he ever had in our forty-nine years was a second-hand car. He spent his entire mustering out pay on the two rings. Oh, I feel like such a fool. You think you know someone."

"Mom! I feel like daddy is here in this room with us - laughing. I can hear him laughing."

"Yes, dear. Like in a crowded room, you knew where he was by his laugh."

"And we always thought we knew daddy like a book. So predictable."

"Your father has had the last laugh and allowed us to join in with him."

And Mrs. Fox and her daughter Marion laughed through their tears listening to Fred's inimitable laughter, from afar yet so near.

DIRTY POOL

Cyril and Stephanie sat on the sofa with their martinis. Behind them the French doors were open to the warm September evening, the terrace and the swimming pool beyond.

Cyril was bulging out of his old blazer after a big dinner. He kept tugging at the lapels. Stephanie examined her skirt like it belonged in a thrift shop.

"Oh, stop fussing, Cyril. We'll get you a new one."

"Is it in the budget?"

"It will be." she dragged on her Dunhill.

"Where's good old George got to, anyway?"

"He wandered off, mumbling to himself."

"You certainly had poor Sally run to her knees tonight, ladling out the vino. Where's she got to, by the way?" he said, examining his empty glass.

"I sent her off. She had a date. She can clean up tomorrow. It's for the Sallies of the world that they still make candlelight and wine. At least someone's getting it on."

"Oh, Sally's a good soul."

"I'm so sick of George's bragging about his wine cellar. His 1951 this and his 1949 that. What the hell's it for if not to drink?" she puffed on her cigarette.

"What was all that fuss about the Olympics at dinner?"

"I couldn't help needling him about his failed attempt to make the diving team. The jackknife." She traced a line above an eyebrow.

"Ancient history. Must be thirty years now."

"That's why he had that damn board put up. Insanity is doing the same thing over and over again and expecting different results. I tell you if I hear that

123

board squeak, squeak, ba-ba-ba-bung once more I'll scream."

"Well, this summer's over. The pool man will be here tomorrow."

"Hmm."

"You know, Stephie, I think it was the business with Marion's jewelry and then the cruise we took that sent George over the top as it were. Estranged us."

"Marion left it to me, her only sister."

"Yes, but you might have waited a bit before you pawned it."

"A decent interval, you mean. You didn't complain when you got your ass into the Sea Cloud bar. You couldn't get rid of that black tie fast enough."

"A black tie puts chaps off. It was lovely, though, first class. Breakfast on a trolley. Met a splendid chap. Said he'd call. Never did. At least people on a boat are broadminded. Don't think anyone noticed."

"Darling, we were all waiting for you to break into the duets from 'Showboat' on the fantail."

"You found tall, dark and handsome soon enough."

Stephie ran a hand through her hair, "Ah, Sashi. Sashi, whatever."

"Still, I don't see why you had to pick up his bar bill. Thought those chaps weren't supposed to drink."

"Yes, Hindus. And we're not supposed to..."

"Yes, yes, I know. The flesh is weak."

"Sashi was a medical student. I helped prepare him for the long hours and catnaps of internship. He was honest, though. Never said he'd call."

Cyril gazed into his glass; "Marion was a good sort. Miss her."

"My God, if you knew how many checks she wrote to lawyers and young men. You must know where every men's room in the city is. You could write a guidebook. We could slip it into packages of Depends. A public service message, wink-wink."

Cyril writhes, "Don't be cruel, Stephie."

"Oh, tosh. It's amazing how you slip into that British accent when you're oiled."

"It's those damned public schools father sent me to. Why couldn't I have just as well gone to school here?"

"Someone told him they'd beat it out of you."

"Little did they know."

"Yes, but you do speak beautifully."

"I say, it was prescient of Marion to wring the promise from George to give you and me an allowance."

"What you can do with a morphine drip and guilt."

"If the bastard had only taken her to that specialist six months sooner, Cyril fumed.

"If only I'd had the foresight to have a cost of living adjustment written into it. I met Tony through George and Marion. George and Tony were supposed to be best buds. Then when the auditors and the IRS came down on them, it was Tony who had signed everything. Then the indictment, that was the closest Tony ever came to sports, shooting himself. And no payoff on suicide. He could have at least driven off a cliff.

"With the station car, of course."

"Of course," Stephanie took a long drag.

"Maybe I should go out and have a look around for George? He was three sheets to the wind."

"Absolutely not! The last time you offered to help, with that flat tire thing, he screamed at you as if it were your fault. You got the hiccups so bad I was up with you all night."

"Oh, that's all forgotten."

"And another thing, I came into the hall this morning to use the phone and when I picked it up, George was on the line, giving Mister Flint holy hell and telling him to be down here tomorrow morning, never mind it was Saturday. That's what a retainer is for. And. And bring a copy of his will along."

"What can that mean?" Cecil leaned in.

"There are only three things you do with a will; write them, change them and execute them."

"Oh, well, none of our business."

Don't say that. The house and the income from the bonds are George's, but revert to you and I on his death."

And by the by, Stephie, what was that wild goose chase you sent George and me on this afternoon. The shipping company could find no record of a delivery for you. Why didn't you just ring them up and tell them to try again?"

"Apparently, they tried three times. That's their limit. I must have gotten the delivery companies mixed up. There are so many of them now. I'll straighten it out."

Cyril and Stephie looked up at the sound, almost a musical phrase, a crunch – crunch and wa wa – wa wa from beyond the terrace.

"I say, Stephie, what was that?"

Stephie patted his hand, "Oh, you know what that sound is, it's the halyard banging against the aluminum flagpole. Cyrie, see what's left in the shaker."

Cyril rose unsteadily and made his way to the drinks tray.

Stephie walked slowly out onto the terrace. In a few moments she returned, pulling her shawl up around her shoulders. "Oh, I knew there was something I had forgotten to tell George. The pool man won't be here tomorrow. Has a wedding to go to."

"So old George will have his pool for another week."

"No. He came today while you were out. I watched him drain it. He had to disconnect the underwater lights too, some sort of short."

Cyril rattled the shaker like a monkey.

Stephie took a deep breath, "No more tonight, Cyrie. We have to be fresh in the morning for the lawyer. Probably have to pick him up at the station. We can drop your old blazer off at Good Will at the same time. Make an appointment at Perry's for a fitting for you."

Stephie picked up a roll of yellow police tape. "And this. The pool man was in such a hurry. I told the poor man I'd string it up around the pool. He left about a foot of water at the bottom with a solution for stain removal. He said with the water he left in the pool, on a moonlit night like this, the pool might appear full from the high board, a false depth perception. Thus the safety tape. The walls of the pool were very stained with the sun tan lotion all his bimboes leave. Well, I'll go out and do it now. Better safe than sorry."

Cyril set down the cocktail shaker and slid out of the room. Stephie stood in the doorway with one hand on the light switch. She looked around the room. "All in all, not a bad summer."

Angie and Tessy Cut Out

"Tessy, get in the car!"

"Angela, what? I just did my nails. Look"

"Fuck your nails! You think I squeal into your driveway like a maniac for nothing? Get in the fucking car now!"

"Awright, awright for Chrissake. I'm coming, all ready. What's the big deal?"

"Lock the door."

"Hey, watch the traffic! You don't even look before you back up."

"Fuck the traffic. We're in deep shit, Tessy. We gotta run for it."

"What? Angie, what is it?"

"I just heard from Ida over at the beauty parlor, they just found Ronnie. She's dead."

"Dead! OhmyGod. What happened?"

"'What happened?' What do you think happened? What did I say was going to happen?"

"Pills? She took pills?"

"They pulled her white Caddy out of Jamaica Bay by Rockaway Boulevard in Queens. Near that bridge that goes to Howard Beach, Cross Bay Boulevard. She was in the trunk, in a plastic bag. It's not even on the news yet. Ida's nephew is a cop. He called her about something else. He told her in passing. They found the car at seven this morning. Some fishermen saw the white car under the water when the sun hit it. Ida knows we're friends of Ronnie's. She's good people. She called me right away."

"It wasn't pills, then?"

"No, Tessy, it wasn't pills. Unless you think she drove the car off the bridge, then climbed into the trunk and into that plastic bag."

"Angie, don't make fun. Hey, how many years I'm asking you to call me Terry, not Tessy?"

"'Terry'. What are you, from Vassar now? Tessy was good enough for grandma, for mama and for you for thirty years. Now all of a sudden you're 'Terry'. Don't put on airs. Listen, we're in deep shit here. We gotta get out of town."

"Angie, where we going? Hey! You almost hit that old lady. Watch it, for Chrissake. So who would pop Ronnie? She never did nothing to nobody. So she drank too much. I'd drink like a fish, too, if I was married to don Utrillo. The stories she told me. What a monster!"

"That's her problem. She told too many tales out of school. It was don Utrillo iced Ronnie. I know it. Remember the barbecue on don Utrillo's lawn in Long Beach in July, the Fourth? Then we went to that joint on the way back to the city that Dom and Johnny were thinking of moving into, the fish place with the nice view of the bay?

"Yeah, yeah, so."

"So, remember the good looking blonde guy with the nice buns who was coming on to you? The Milanese? In the parking lot? Dom and Johnny got into a fight with him? They beat the shit out of him? Threw him in that dumpster with the fish heads?"

"Remember Dom said, 'How appropriate in his sharkskin suit.'"

"Very funny. But they picked on the wrong guy this time. The guy died. He was connected. He was the nephew of don Benny, from New York."

"Don Benedetto from the Christmas Party in Little Italy last Christmas?"

"Yeah. Don Benny and don Utrillo are like oil and water. They don't mix. I seen this coming. Somebody kills his nephew; he's not going to let it

129

pass. He's got to have revenge. Even if he don't like the guy, he's got to take action. His position, you understand?"

"Don Benny killed Ronnie?"

"No! You don't listen. Ronnie knew about the fight at the restaurant. She was talking too much, about a lot of other things, too. She was leading don Benny to don Utrillo and by extension to Dom and Johnny. If don Utrillo pops his wife to cover his ass what do you think those two weasels, your Johnny and my Dom would do to us to save their skins?"

"Oh, Angie, not Johnny. He wouldn't do that to me. I can't believe it. He loves me. I know it. I feel it."

"Yeah. Between the sheets you feel it. Tessy, listen to me. I'm your sister, right? I always looked after you, right? Did I ever steer you wrong? Did I get us out of that crummy job in the chorus?"

"Yeah, yeah, all that. But how do you know what they plan? What they're going to do? I can't believe this. Where we going? Where are you going?"

"We're going to Manhattan. How do I know? How do I know? When Tina didn't get off the school bus from Saint Rose's I called the principal, Sister Benignus. She said Dom picked up Tina. They talked. She knows him from grammar school. He was taking Tina to her grandmother's for the weekend, he said. I said I must have got my dates mixed up. I smelled a rat. Dom would never do that without telling me. It's not like him. He knows I'd scream if I didn't know where she was. But I wouldn't be around to scream if Dom had his way, would I? No, we're being set up, Tessy. Believe me. I feel it in my bones. You can't be married to these guys all these years and not see the signs. I got out of the house fast. I've had a bag packed for years, anyway.

130

They thought they still had time, see. They didn't know about Ida. They didn't count on Ida. See, this is Friday, right? What do we do every Friday?"

"Go to the Cabana Club. They meet us later. We eat. Like always."

"That long empty stretch of road between the dunes on the way to the Club? Make it look like a robbery. You know, whata you call it, a car-jacking. See, it comes back to me. One time we're coming home on that lonely stretch and Dom says, 'Hey, what a spot to stretch some guy, nice and quiet.' Like you always go alone in your little Triumph and I always go in this boat 'cause I can't stand those little cars. Last night Dom says to me, 'Pick up your sister tomorrow for the spa 'cause her car is on the fritz. Then youse can go together to the Club in the afternoon. See? Two birds with one stone. Nobody to talk to the cops or don Benny's people."

"I just had the Triumph tuned-up. Runs like a top. I was driving it last night."

"I bet if you tried it right now it wouldn't start."

"I still can't believe it. O.K., Dom is a prick but not Johnny."

"Grow up, Tessy. The apple doesn't fall far. Johnny does what ever Dom tells him. Dom says 'shit', little brother Johnny says, 'What color?' What? Stop crying. So the party's over. Get out with our skins. Shut up."

"I still can't believe it, Angie. I mean, the house, our lives. What are we going to do? Where we going? Where can we go they won't find us? I don't even have a pocketbook with me. My credit cards. My clothes. Oh my God, the safety deposit box! The money. In the bank. Angie, we got to go back."

"No. No going back for nothing. Look. By now Johnny or Dom called to keep tabs on us. Nobody answers. They smell a rat. They have the bank watched. Ida's. Mama's. From now on everything is cash. No credit cards. They can trace the credit cards. Where you bought gas, a motel. You leave a paper trail, they follow. From now on strictly cash. Give me a token from the tray. Well, Tessy slash Terry, kiss Brooklyn goodbye."

"Can't we even call mama? She'll worry."

"We'll send her a card. She'll understand. She wasn't born yesterday, like some people."

"What about Tina? How could you leave her, your daughter?"

"Could you see her with us? Running like rats."

"Still. Oh, my God, what are we going to do, Angie?"

"In my bag. Take a Valium. It'll be OK. You leave it to Angie. I'm not about to let these pricks throw dirt in our faces. Here's the Bus Depot. Look at these skags. This place is like a magnet for these scumbags. We'll park here."

"You can't park here. It says, 'Tow Away Zone'. We'll be towed."

"Good. We can't use this car anymore anyway. Stands out like a sore thumb. I had to have it painted blushing pink. There's not two cars like this in New York, I bet. By this time Dom has an A.P.B. out on the car. Make the cops do his work for him."

"We're taking a bus? Where to?"

"Where would you like to go, Tessy?"

"Miami. I always like Miami. We know people there. Tommy G., maybe he'd help us?"

"Maybe, good idea. I'll get two tickets to Miami. Hold my suitcase. Guard it with your life."

"What took you so long? But, now don't get mad, Angie. I called mama. I just couldn't leave without telling her something. I had to Ange."

"I understand. What did you tell her?"

"I told her we got domestic troubles. We were going to Florida, but I didn't say where. I didn't say Miami."

"What did she say?"

"Oh, she cried, you know. She said she understood. I told her we'd call when we got somewhere. OK?"

"Sure. Relax. Wait here. I just want to see what the bus looks like. Get us good seats. Don't move and don't let go of that bag."

"Angie! Where's your purse? Isn't that our bus they're announcing, 'Last call.'? Angie, the Miami bus is leaving! What the fuck's going on here?"

"Tessy, be quiet before I slap you. Now calm down and listen to me. Anybody starts snooping around finds we bought two tickets to Miami, right? Then I walk through the bus and sit next to the sleaziest character I can find. I remember a call I have to make. I run off the bus. I leave my purse behind. I miss the bus, right? The sleaze can't believe his luck. He goes through the bag. Takes the credit cards. He has a field day between here and Philadelphia, and Baltimore, and Washington and wherever he's going. He forges my name or his girlfriend does. They leave a paper trail for Dom and Johnny to follow."

"But then they'll know we're going to Miami. What good did all this do?"

"Are we on the bus, Tessy?"

"No, but."

"But my ass. Come on. Follow me. We're taking the subway downtown. We'll stop at a couple of stores. We'll get our hair done. I think I'll go back to black or what used to be black. No more of this henna. And a short cut for summer. No more bleach

133

for you. We'll eighty-six the leopard skin toreadors, lose the hoop earings. We'll go to K-Mart. Ever been to K-Mart? By the time I'm through with us, we'll look like L.L. Bean's daughters.

"Hey, Angie, I didn't know there was a railroad station under Madison Square Garden! Cool. You don't have to get wet if it rains. Remember the time we came here for the fights? Dom owned that little Filipino fighter. He lost. Wonder what happened to him? Never saw him again. Where we going? Where'd you get tickets for?"

"I'll tell you on the train. The fighter went home to the Philippines. Let me look at you. You look good,different."

"Angie, I'm starving. I gotta eat. Let's get pizza."

"No time. They just posted our platform. Follow me. We'll eat on the train. They got a dining car. Go in front of me. I'll show the guy the tickets. I can feel those guys looking for us. They're pricks but they're not stupid. Remember that. Miami! You little jerk. They'll wheedle Miami out of mama, don't worry. Dom will tell her he can't protect us unless he knows where we are. He'll make it sound like it's don Benny is after us, not him. He's smooth. He's persuasive. That's why he's a capo."

"Hey, these seats are comfortable. So, where we going, Angie?"

"Talk low. Here, look at your ticket, 'Rosemary Morris'."

"Buffalo! What's in Buffalo for crissake? And who's this Rosemary Morris?"

"Tessy, can't you talk low? We're tourists going to Buffalo. In the summer tourists go to Buffalo. We got Reserved Seating. Guarantees a seat. On this train you got no choice. It's all reserved. When you buy reserved, even for cash you gotta give them a name.

But you don't gotta show I.D. See? Look at mine. 'Kathleen Turner'."

"Hey, like the actress. Who's Rosemary Morris?"

"Who cares? It's a name. It's as far away as I could get from Tessy Balsalmo at the time. You don't have to remember it. It's just temporary. From Buffalo we take a bus to the Falls. From the Falls we go visit Canada. Then another bus to Toronto. I got a friend in Toronto. Somebody Dom and Johnny don't even know. She'll get us papers. It'll cost us but we got it right here. We'll fade. We'll disappear. We'll survive. If you start crying on me again, I swear I'll smack you. Just remember Ronnie all wrinkled and blue in the trunk. Come on. I got us down for the first seating. Let's eat."

GOING DOWN

"Hold it, pal! This is a freight elevator only, no passengers. Go around front to the passenger elevators."

"Yes, I know. But I'm in a bit of a fix. I wonder if you could help me out. It's all rather embarrassing. There's a process server camped out in front of my office. Some silly misunderstanding with my ex-wife. You know how vindictive they can be. The alimony check is a day late and they have a breakdown. I'm with Lodge, Stein and Brennan. "

"Who?"

"The investment firm on fourteen. They have half the floor."

"So what are you doing on thirteen?"

"That's what I'm trying to explain. It's so embarrassing. A grown man slinking around. My God, at my age. Our offices have a back door to the back stairs. I skipped out when the receptionist buzzed me. We had a sign if anybody difficult came calling. Glad I didn't forget her for Christmas."

"So you lost the guy. Take the regular passenger elevator. Hey, if the boss sees me taking people up and down in this thing, I get suspended. There are all kinds of insurance regulations about people in freight elevators. And this crate ain't working all that great to begin with, something wrong with the electrical switches. It don't stop when you want it to. Stops between floors. Shit like that."

"Yes, I can see you have your problems. But if you would just listen to me for a moment. By the way, Scott Chadwick, Lodge, Stein and Brennan, investment brokers, and you?"

"Paul, Pauly Kinsella. Hi."

"How do you do, Pauly? Listen, Pauly. You married? Got any children?"

"Yeah. I got three kids. So?"

"It's just that being a parent yourself I feel sure you'll see my difficulty. Where to begin?"

"Look pal, I can't stand here all day, you know?"

"Of course, of course, Pauly. I can see you're a man of affairs. To be perfectly frank, it's not a process server I'm avoiding. It's the authorities."

"What? The cops?"

"Yes. The police. Oh, it's all such a mix-up. Her attorney won't take my attorney's calls. Everyone's on an ego trip."

"So, they can't lock you up for alimony anymore. They did away with that law."

"To be sure, Pauly. But this is child support payments. She swore out a warrant, the bitch. What I ever saw in her. I sent the check to the school for the tuition but my secretary drew it on the wrong account. My personal checking is a little low. The check bounced. But I have the cash with me. That's where I was heading when Velma buzzed me. At least she can do something right. See? That's why I have my luggage with me. I'm on my way up to the Academy to straighten it all out and visit my son."

"What Academy?"

"Faircliff. Faircliff Academy for future leaders, the brochure said. Don't you see, Pauly? If the police arrest me, there's all the paperwork, the attorneys running back and forth. It's not jail. My God, I'd spend a night in jail anytime for my son, wouldn't you? Of course you would, Pauly. But that won't get the fees up to Faircliff any sooner, will it? This way, if I can just get to my car in the basement. It's so embarrassing for Scott, Jr., suspended from all his classes until the bill is paid. Do you believe these

137

mercenary bastards? Why, I went to Faircliff. My father went to Faircliff. Well, if I could just get out of the building. You do see my position, Pauly?"

"Aw'right, aw'right. You're breaking my heart. Get on. But stay in the back behind the dry wall. If anybody comes, duck down."

"Thanks Pauly. You're a prince. Rather dusty back here, isn't it?"

"That's why they call it a freight elevator."

"Can we go directly to the parking level? I'm in rather a hurry, as you may well imagine."

"I gotta make a stop on three. Dump off this electrical stuff. The electrician will be waiting for it. So stay down when the door opens. Don't brush against the wall with that coat. Nice coat. Must have gone for 350 - 400 bucks for that?"

"Nine hundred, actually."

"Nine hundred bucks for a coat!"

"Yes. I should have gone for the velvet collar. Only two hundred more. Getting prudent in my old age."

"Yeah, prudent. My brother's divorced. Two kids. Very messy. I don't blame him he takes a drink with that bitch. They got along for years, one day she announces she's going to college. Forty years old, she's gotta go back to school. She's gotta find herself. Believe this shit? She throws him out. So he had a girlfriend on the side. She got her house money regularly. The kids had shoes, know what I mean?"

"Of course, your brother is just a man of the world."

"He's no saint. Don't get me wrong. I don't go along with everything he done. Like buying the boat without telling her, with the money they had put aside for the extension on the house. That was too much.

But she took him to the cleaners. I don't blame him for staying out of work. He should break his ass. She gets half of his take home. And all she does is go to school. Lucky the kids are in high school. They can take care of themselves."

"Aren't we going rather slowly?"

"I told you they're working on the electrical panel. That's why I gotta drop off this stuff for the electricians on three. So what do you drive, Scotty?"

"I have a Jaguar now. An X-6."

"A Jaguar, not too shabby. Nice. I got a Ranger."

"A Ranger? I don't believe I know that one."

"A Ranger, Ford Ranger. Like a small pickup. But I got the cap."

"Just what is a cap?"

"It's a top they put over the bed to enclose it. You never seen a Ranger?"

"I don't believe I've had the pleasure."

"Two years old. Had thirty thousand on it, but it runs good. Gets me to work and back."

"What the hell was that?"

"We stalled. It's nothing. Don't worry about it. It does that. Now if this phone is working, I'll call downstairs. See what the hold up is."

"Are we safe? Is it safe?"

"Sometimes the cable gets crossed on the drum or there's a short. This is probably a short. See, the elevator thinks you want it to stop. Don't worry. -- Hello, who's this? Fittzy? Pauly. Listen, Fittzy, what happened? Electrical. I figured. Fittzy, where's the boss? He went on his break; to the Blarney Stone, I bet. Listen, don't leave me hanging here. I got a pregnant lady on the elevator. No, no, I'm only kidding. But I do have a passenger. Hey, don't tell me about the rules. I came here when they were written on the bark of a tree. The guy's in a bind. His

139

wife's trying to have him locked up. I'm trying to get him down to the parking level. Yeah, fourteen. Now, I'd say I'm stuck between seven and eight. Forget three. Just get me down to the garage, o.k. Ten minutes? You better not be lying to me, Fittzy. Remember, I'm your ride home to Levittown. O.k., we're waiting. -- You heard. Ten minutes. So, Scotty, I guess you do pretty good in the stock market. Jaguar, cashmere coat, Rolex. Wish I could find a good sound stock for my old age, you know?"

"Have anything in mind? Maybe I could suggest something."

"A friend of mine got into this real estate thing, Rainbow Rancho. He sends them so much each month and in five years he owns this plot in New Mexico."

"O Lord, Pauly. Stay away from Rancho Rainbow. Better you should invest in a leper colony."

"Yeah, why? What's wrong with it?"

"I shouldn't be saying but Rainbow Rancho is going belly up."

"Yeah? My friend says everyday in the papers the stock goes up. He says he's going to buy even more if they let him."

"Well, tell him don't. Put your money back in the mattress, Pauly. When the market opens on Monday morning, Rainbow Rancho is going to drop like a stone. Trust me."

"Yeah? How can you be so sure? I mean, I know you're in the business and all, but I can't just tell my friend a guy on the freight elevator gave me a tip, right?"

"Listen, Pauly. My firm has a controlling block of Rainbow Rancho. We've been buying it up all over town. That makes the price go up. Follow me?"

"Yeah."

"Then when we get the price up to what the market will bear, we sell it, dump it. We sell high. Dump the stock. The price falls. See?"

"Yeah, but ain't that illegal or something?"

"Only if you get caught. It's like arson, very hard to prove intent. The Securities and Exchange Commission investigators, if you can call them that, are rather obtuse and slow off the mark. We bury them in red tape. Their lawyers went to CCNY, ours went to Harvard."

"Intent? What is this intent?"

"Intent is you knowingly manipulated the market in direct violation of the stock market rules and the S.E.C. Regulations. Rules were made to be broken, right?"

"Right. Boy, you guys know all the angles."

"Oh, it's a gift, Pauly. It's a gift."

"So you went to this place Harvard?"

"Certainly did. B.S.S '85, M.B.A. '87. Hey, we're moving."

"Yeah. -- Fittzy? Yeah. At least the phone's working good. You taking me all the way down? Good." "We stopped again. Why did we stop?"

"End of the line, Scotty. We're here."

"Who are these people? What is this?"

"Just some gentlemen from the S.E.C. They'd like to talk to you over at the Federal Building, Scotty."

"What is this? I want to call my attorney? Pauly, who the hell are you? You're not going to tell them what I just said in the elevator? Besides, whatever I said is uncorroborated."

"Yeah, I know. That's why I kept the talk button down in the elevator."

"Nobody can listen in on my conversations without my permission. I know the law."

"Oh, you know the law, Scotty. And so do we. That's why we got a court ordered wire tap on you."

"One thing, Pauly, where did you learn to operate an elevator?"

"CCNY. See you around, Scotty. 'Going up!'

THE MONSIGNOR AND THE MENDICANT

I accompanied my wife on a business trip to D.C. one weekend last summer. While she was doing the Lord's work of trying to get money out of Caesar for the poor I went to Mass in the cathedral from which the chosen are baptized with platinum spoons, married with pre-nup trust funds and buried with glowing obits.

On the way to church in the oppressive heat I passed a restaurant advertising eggs benedict for five dollars. I made a note to breakfast there later.

St. Matt's was a granite temple with broad steps rising high off the hot sidewalk. Its columns and entablature reminded me of the New York Stock Exchange façade. The massive bronze doors opened with a touch as an old lady tottered inside. I saw by the Mass Schedule that I was early. I stood for a moment on the sidewalk under a shade tree off to the side. A man in a black cassock was sweeping the steps of confetti, probably from a Saturday wedding. I assumed he was a sub-deacon. I have never seen a priest shake hands with a broom.

About thirty feet away lounged a small group of men in tattered and filthy clothes. One raised a bottle to his lips as others stood like chicks in the nest with beaks agape, eagerly waiting their turn at the magic elixir, having gotten beyond Wine Tasting 101: sniff, swirl, sip. One man detached himself and slid along the polished granite wall towards me. The sweeper glared at him and said to me, shaking his head, "Don't give him anything."

All this while fashionably dressed couples; crested blazers with Italian straw hats, flowing silk prints and linen and shantung jackets alighted from Jags,

143

Beemers, Mercedes', a vintage MG, and an Aston Martin in the parking lot, clutching Louis Vuitton bags and snapping on Gucci sunglasses to mask their concern for those less fortunate.

The man came up to me. I took a half step back. His nappy hair was matted, possibly dried blood. One leaking eye was closed and discolored, pussy yellow, eggplant purple and black. His few well-spaced teeth were caramel colored. His lip was split. Still, he managed a grin. He wore a maroon ribbed sweater and brown corduroy pants, stained with life on the streets. He sloshed around in tan shoes with string for shoelaces. He held out a palm in a tentative gesture while the other lightly strummed his stomach. I hesitated only a moment. I fished in my pocket and gave him a dollar.

He said, "God bless you, sir. God bless you." and gently taking the bill turned away.

The sweeper stood above me on a step, shaking his head. "He'll only buy drink with that."

Who the hell was he to tell me how to be charitable? I felt rather righteous.

Latecomers trotted up the steps. I followed. Deliciously cool air escaped as the bronze door pivoted open almost as effortlessly one could imagine as the stone across the tomb.

In small, poor parishes the scent of beeswax and incense vie with pine oil and ammonia. Here it was a hint of brass polish, lemon oil and that trace of your grandmother's face powder that we smell on money.

Somewhere hidden from our ears a large central air conditioning unit worked its magic. What must it have cost to cool so vast a chamber? Behind the altar stretched the choir with its opposing parliamentary benches, a hint of the Anglican. Tall stained glass windows pierced the walls. Famous

American Catholic family names modestly announced their gift at the bottom of each window. What was that about, 'Anonymous giving'?

The celebrant was a doddering bishop, bent under hisembroidered chasuble, assisted about the altar by the sweeper deacon. Seated to one side in a carved, high backed chair sat a monsignor, somber, watchful, patient.

When after the opening prayers the bishop was maneuvered onto his scarlet cushion, the monsignor rose and strode to the pulpit. He adjusted the light, took a handkerchief from his sleeve and swiped at his gold-rimmed spectacles. A hush fell over the faithful.

After reading the gospel, along the lines of "Whatever you do to the least of my sisters and brothers, you do to Me.", Monsignor told a golf joke that flew over my head into the nearest water trap. A chuckle floated across the pews. He smiled modestly, acknowledging someone in the first pew with a knowing, raised eyebrow. He glanced at the ceiling, light bouncing off his thin gold rims, his black widow's peak cleaving a high, tanned forehead, picking out the matinee idol jaw line. He wore a snow-white Irish linen surplice lovingly fashioned by cloistered nuns, (size 42 long), and cut low enough to reveal the rose piping and buttons of the monsignorial cassock. I looked at my watch. There was no rustling in the pews, no snapping of purses, no squirming. The monsignor stepped away from the pulpit, adjusting his portable mike and paced to the middle of the stage-altar, a mosaic icon of blue, red and gold chips boarded by Carrara marble. He steepled his tanned fingers, resting his index fingers under his full lower lip and paused.

My stomach growled.

He turned towards his audience and with a modest shooting of linen cuffs, a gold cufflink catching a glint from the nearest Tiffany chandelier, he casually dropped his arms to his sides, palms turned out, readying an appealing gesture. "I've prepared a short sermon and a long sermon. Which would you like to hear?" Modest chuckling came from the pews.

The ancient celebrant had slipped into the arms of Morphius.

"We must remind ourselves that Jesus came among us not to show us how to die but how to live our everyday lives. Every day of His public life was a blueprint for us to live by. Remember, God is not a person and heaven is not a place."

Some heads came up.

"You can always send Him, Her, It an E-mail straight from the heart. Every act we do or fail to do every day of our lives is either selfish or unselfish. We don't need reams of Canon Law to tell us the difference."

This man should be made to carry an Actors' Equity Card.

"This much we do know; life is a limited time offer, selfish or unselfish? And we all have to do our own math."

I was faint with hunger.

The homilist left center stage quickly and resumed his vice-regal seat. The audience exhaled. The ushers with the self-assurance of fencing masters slid long handled wicker baskets through the pews with rapier-like precision. Envelopes and checks modestly folded so as not to inspire envy, fluttered like manna into the green baize lined baskets. A tall altar boy tugged at the lace sleeve of the celebrant who rose and tottered to the altar for the Offertory.

During Communion I noticed the monsignor had fled. During the final hymn, people started to slip out the back. I joined them.

The monsignor stood on the top step in his cassock, surrounded by two middle-aged couples. One woman in a straw hat with a pale blue ribbon rested a hand on his forearm. She gasped, "Tom, you must come to the Club today. This heat!" .

The men stood back, beaming. He was one of them, same prep school, same stock portfolio, same golf club, shot in the middle 70's, took a drink.

A tall man with receding hair added "They have a new chef." A round man lighting a thin Havana, "They've moved all the holes." The short woman, "I'm going to float in that pool until I'm water-logged."

The monsignor smiled, "Believe it or not, Sunday is a busy day for me. I'll try to get out there during the week."

I stood on the sidewalk and looked around. The mendicants were gone, resting between Masses. I made my way to the restaurant and ate eggs benedict, fresh ground hazelnut coffee fresh squeezed orange juice, 'bread baked on the premises.' Listening to these priests who had never missed a meal in their lives telling the rest of us how to spend our money always made me hungry.

On the way back to my hotel, the breakfast I had so greedily consumed now turning against me as I staggered through the rising humid heat waves. I came up behind and almost joined a long line of shabbily dressed men and some women shuffling their way through the oppressive heat. I almost crossed the street when I noticed they were filing through a large, wrought iron gateway into the rear yard of the cathedral. They climbed down a flight of stairs. I went closer and peered through the iron railings. Below me was an outdoor soup kitchen of sorts, long tables of food and stacks of plates. The hungry piled trays with rolls, cereal, juice cartons, plates of scrambled eggs, like a Christmas scene from Dickens. Servers stood behind the tables dishing out food. And there was the monsignor in a loud Hawaiian shirt, dishing out sausage links, shucking and jiving, "You the man." He pointed his spatula at the man I had given the dollar to. The mendicant replied, "No. You the man. God bless you, Father."

I drifted back towards my hotel, reflecting, had I truly given the man the dollar out of charity or was it guilt, or defiance of authority? Had I not slandered the monsignor in my heart for being a man who knew his audiences, a man who had learned to push the rich man through the eye of the needle, and got him to cut his cloak in half and like it?

THE UNDERTAKER'S APPRENTICE

When I landed in Korea in the middle of March 1953, the snow was gone, leaving mud, which froze at night in the trenches around brown footprints of boondockers and Mickey Mouse Boots. Cocoa colored comm wire was stapled along the sides of the shale trenches. The shoelace hooks of the Mickey Mouse boots were forever catching on the comm wire. You had to resist jerking them loose.

We were strung along the main trench on a ridge, three and four to a sandbagged bunker. Before us was the Outpost, (OP) a small hill about a half-mile in front, manned by a platoon. Down the hill behind us was the Company C.P., and behind that, Battalion and Regiment, and Division where we were told they had a choice of movies. Enemy mortars probed the rear looking for ammo or fuel dumps. Our biggest worry was snipers; stay down, keep moving.

When I was there about ten days, the O.P. was attacked at sundown, pounded to a pulp and overrun by 11 p.m. Three days later it was retaken. All day we carried groaning stretchers down from the Gate, an opening in the concertina wire that led out front to a trail down to a dyke, wound across a collection of grey, barren rice paddies and finally up a steep trail to the circular trenched O.P.

The O.P. was secured by noon. The wounded were carried quickly to the rear. Stretcher-bearers were either trudging up hill or slip-sliding down hill. Because of the steep terrain, the Marines were lashed to the stretchers with battle bandages and comm wire. Bearers stumbled and fell, sliding down the greasy clay sides of the dykes. As the afternoon wore on the dead were finally carried in.

Forward Med was a clearing where senior Corpsman triaged the wounded. The incoming shelling had been so heavy that APC's- Armored Personnel Carriers- were sent up in daylight to evac the wounded instead of ambulances. There were two rows of stretchers on one side of the road. The row in front was to be shipped out first. The second row was just hanging on. While waiting for transport, Corpsman stood holding aloft bottles of albumen or lashing them to upturned rifle butts, their barrels bayoneted into the ground. A thin beige tube ran down into a pale arm. The second row had the same pink and red bandages, the same albumen. A haggard Corpsman passed among them, pausing here and there, tapping or pinching a peach fuzzed, ashen cheek, checking eyes, pulses, the manila Railway Express-like card tied to each top buttonhole. The squeezed flat olive drab syrettes of quarter grain morphine were stuck into lapels like miniature toothpaste tubes. With the stroke of a stubby pencil, a Corpsman would scratch out a notation on the card and add a new one with a new time. Then he would stand and motion us to move the stretcher across the road.

Across the road was a row of quiet stretchers with forms now only suggested under green blankets or camouflaged ponchos. It was called poncho rotation. Someone's pride and joy, whether hell raiser or saint, rich or poor, now forever equal. Pairs of boots stuck out from under the stained blankets, muddy boots, leaning inboard and outboard, the mud dry now on earlier arrivals, still wet on latecomers. On one stretcher, only one foot stuck out. One pair of boots was so new, the size in silver paint shone from the soles.

The random shelling stopped around the clearing and along the road to the rear. Ambulances appeared and the possibles were taken away. More stretchers were called for up at the Gate, and the dead were gently removed from theirs. They were allowed to keep their blankets and ponchos.

We climbed back up the hill, each carrying a folded stretcher, sweating in our field jackets with winter liners. The sun was warm, the sky blue, the air stirred with spring.

As the sun dropped behind the hills, the cold returned, the mud froze. We were sent back to our squads. My bunker was empty. Mahoney had been hit by mortar fire four days earlier and Oakhurst had been wounded in the arm. Their stuff had been taken away; the Willy-Peter bags, mini sea bags we kept strapped to pack boards with comm wire, cigar boxes of letters and photos. The two empty racks stripped of sleeping bags were made of comm wire strung across barbed wire stakes.

I couldn't remember how long I had been in Korea. When I first got to the bunker and we heard a round coming in, Mahoney had taught me to place a hand across the top of my canteen cup to keep out the sand that rained down from the sandbagged roof when the round hit.

Cpl. Mullins stuck his head in between the overlapping blankets nailed across the doorway. A supply truck had just pulled into the C.P. with ammo and 'C' rations. One man from each squad for unloading, junior man, etc.

At the company H.Q. all the stretchers were gone. A light rain washed over the day. Some men wore ponchos, most didn't bother. We unloaded the small pine boxes of .30 caliber ammo and color-coded boxes of 'C' rations. Like gold, the ammo boxes were deceptively heavy. In the truck's headlights we made three stacks, one for each platoon. Other Marines trooped down the trails with pack boards and staggered back up with cans of water or ammo or food on their backs. The empty truck pulled away.

Take a break but don't get lost. We stood in clusters, shoulders hunched against the rain, glowing cigarettes cupped under the cuffs of sodden field jackets. The aroma of Navy coffee drifted from a sagging mess tent that had been used during the day as a first aid clearing station. A chink of golden light slipped through the tent flaps.

After the rush for coffee was over, I drifted into the tent just to stop the incessant drumming of the rain on my helmet. On one side a glowing Coleman lantern stood hissing on a plywood counter. A sergeant stood behind it doing paperwork. On the right, in the yellow cone of the lantern, two Marines sat on the ground, backs against the tent wall, smoking, hands folded over steaming canteen cups, legs stretched out, ankles crossed. The lantern glow picked up by the mud on their boots. Around the edge of the tent, Marines squatted or knelt on one knee, sipping coffee, smoking, chatting softly about the day, about someone who got hit, baseball, home. The rain hummed on the tent.

Another truck pulled up with hooded headlights. Everybody out!

Like zombies, we moved from the tailgate to the stacks and back again, plopping through the rain and mud. After awhile, you can no longer distinguish between wet and dry. You are wet all over, inside and out, rain and sweat now one.

When that truck rumbled its way out of the muddy clearing, the men squatted on the ammo boxes. The rain slowed. Some lit up. Most sat hunched against a rain that could do them no more harm.

I went back into the tent. The sergeant looked nice and dry. The two Marines who had sat against the tent wall were gone. Two at the back of the tent, whom I had noticed earlier, their crossed, muddy boots glistening at the edge of the lamplight, were still there. I was soaked through, weary, and put upon, not reasoning out how you got not to be the junior man in your squad in a war.

"Hey, why can't these guys pitch in? They've been here for hours."

The sergeant raised the lantern above his head, its widened circle revealing the two Marines, "Because their dead."

They lay stretched out, their arms at their sides, bare headed, manila tags tied to the field jackets. No bandages, no blood. It must have been quick. One, his head cocked to the side, awaiting a silent order. Shrapnel can come the size of that lopsided ashtray you made in shop, a postage stamp, half a broken pencil or one of mom's sewing needles.

The sergeant stared at me for a moment. "We're waiting for an ambulance." Then he mercifully lowered the lamp.

I left.

Outside, I took off my helmet, raising my burning face up to the cooling rain. I began to hyperventilate, then calmed down. I went back to unloading the next truck.

Had the ammo boxes become lighter? What was wrong with a little rain? After all, it was officially spring. I had tomorrow. I had options.

A Train at Night

Once, while stationed at the Brooklyn Navy Yard, I was assigned as a brig chaser to go up to Buffalo with a sergeant to pick up a deserter being held in the Erie County Jail for non-support. I was an eager young corporal and Sergeant Pakula had a reputation for going wild when he drank. He had a Silver Star, a Bronze Star and two Purple Hearts. The story went that at the Inchon landing he beat a gook to death with a C-ration can when he ran out of ammo. I think the captain sent me along as a civilizing influence.

With government tickets and some cash we left Penn Station about 1800 hours, (that's 6 p.m.). We had Pullman berths. The train crossed under the Hudson and chugged across Jersey as we ate in the drab dining car. The Pullman and Dining Car were pre-war. The Pennsy and the Central were well into their slide against the airlines. The stiff, musty chairs were covered in worn, dull green baize. We crossed the Delaware and turned north through Pennsylvania and back into New York through the hilly Appalachians. Once, we passed ourselves on a switchback.

The sergeant opened a briefcase containing our 45's, arm bands, cuffs and a file on the deserter. He was a sergeant from the Third Air Wing in Florida! What could be cushier, I thought, thinking of my fourteen months in Korea in the infantry?

We were met with a car at the station in Buffalo at 0700 by a young lieutenant from the recruiting station in the downtown Buffalo General Post Office. He was dressed in undressed Blues and clearly disliked this seamier side of Marine Corps life. On the way out of town he filled us in. What had happened was when the Corps was notified of the deserter's arrest for non-support, the lieutenant was sent to the hearing. He asked the judge that the deserter be turned over to them for Court Martial and that they would deal far more harshly with him than Erie County. The lady judge said no dice, "You guys will just give him a slap on the wrist." She gave him six months on the county farm.

When he was first picked up he was still only A.W.O.L.but after thirty days it was desertion. At that time, the government had adopted a new undeclared policy of not chasing all around the country for guys over the hill since F.B.I. statistics had shown that most returned before the thirty day mark and the expenditures were not justified. If this guy hadn't been picked up by the local police he'd still be loose. Fortunately we were not at war but the six months would still be tacked onto his crime.

I remember during a mortar barrage, a guy saying he wished he was back in the brig, where he was safe.

The deserter had discontinued the allotment to his wife on his own. Government policy in this country was to stop the pay of deserters but continue the allotment for dependents. Not so in Canada for instance. In Korea I rode on a train with some Canadians just out of the stockade.

It was a cold and windy February day under a grey sky. The Prison Farm was surrounded by the stubble of a corn field, the rows lined with light snow. We waited in the quiet, poorly lit lobby, listening to an old pendulum clock on the wall above ornate radiators hissing against the wainscoted walls.

The deserter was led into the room in cuffs and up to the desk. He wore a wrinkled blue suit that looked like it had stood in the window long after the sale was

155

over. I had expected him to be in uniform, a sergeant in the Air Wing! In Florida no less! The lieutenant handled the paperwork, signing off on the prisoner. Sgt. Pakula stood off to the side, measuring the deserter.

Before our train had arrived at Buffalo, while we were eating breakfast, Sergeant Pakula had said, "Never mind whatever this recruiting officer tells you. Here's the way we're going to do this; I'll cuff him to my left wrist. You stay behind us at all times so he never knows just where you are. If he makes a grab for my gun, club him. If he is un-cuffed and makes a run for it, kill him. I'm not coming back to the Yard empty handed."

The deserter was about six feet tall, short blond hair, nice looking guy, a poster Marine. When he saw us standing there in our greens with the red and gold arm bands his eyes lit up. He was glad to see us before he realized what was happening, like sometimes when you see the flag.

The lieutenant dropped us off at the station, glad to be rid of this seamy side of the job.

In the station I walked behind Sergeant Pakula and the deserter, carrying the briefcase. The deserter stopped when he saw the diner, smelling the coffee and eggs frying, "Hey! Can we stop? I'm dying for some real chow. They don't even give you salt in there. I have money. Can we? I'm buying." It was like we were all away at camp and he wanted to join our gang.

Sergeant Pakula looked up at the board. I said, "I could go for coffee."

We sat at the counter. There were few people about at that hour. The waitress in a strawberry blond beehive looked at us as if to say she had seen it all. Pakula and I had coffee. He had ham and eggs. We watched him eat, the waitress, too. He ate the pattern off the plate, not a crumb was lost. She brought him extra toast. Pakula made a face as if to say, you'll spoil him.

The deserter had a small gym bag which he carried after Pakula examined its contents. They sat in coach seats with me behind them. The deserter had a checker set and he and Pakula played for much of the dull ten hour trip back to New York.

As we passed slowly through the switching yards of red and yellow lights, he said, "Look! That's my house." I half expected a teary eyed couple to come out on the sooty grey back porch and wave tear stained handkerchiefs at us.

The deserter told us how last summer his mother wrote him in Florida to say his wife was running around with her old boyfriend. They had no children. When he went over the hill, he went home and lived with his parents. His father got him a job in the steel mill where he worked, until he was arrested. I remembered the bunker I had been in last July and the pounding we took, the sand drizzling down our necks from the sand bags overhead where the stitching had burst, like someone tapping you on the shoulder to say, don't go away, there's more.

The deserter was saying, "I know I was stupid. But I just couldn't stand the idea of supporting that bitch. I kept my uniform pressed on a hanger behind the front door. I knew it was only a matter of time before you caught me. She saw me in town, Gloria, and swore out a warrant against me for non-support. I didn't think I would wind up in the County Jail and that they wouldn't let me wear my uniform."

Once, un-cuffing the prisoner to allow him to go to the head, Pakula looked over his shoulder at me as he bent to unlock the cuffs. I flicked the safety off my

45. The deserter's head moved as he heard the click.

At the Brooklyn Navy Yard they had the custom of standing a prisoner before all those assembled outside the mess hall at noon chow, waiting for the doors to open and reading out the results of someone's Court Martial. It's analogous to holding ticker tape parades on Broadway during the lunch hour. A month after the train trip the deserter stood at attention in the sun, his face thinner, his hair shorn, in soiled dungarees, head uncovered.

When I had first heard of his rank and cushy duty I was envious of the deserter. But what was his crime really? His wife was running free, his parents were heart-broken, and he was marked for life. He had been crushed and wanted to go home. Hadn't I learned in Korea that the heritage of war is that it is a place where you lose things and they don't let you go home at night? Our eyes met. I looked away.

The Irish Thrush

In 1883, when I was twelve and Jimmy my younger brother was eight, our father died of the consumption and mother, after several letters from across the sea in New York, reluctantly agreed to leave Ireland and go out to America. Bill and Marty, my elder brothers, had gone out to America four years earlier and Frank and Joe followed in two years. On receiving word that our dada had died, Bill wrote that since we owned no land nor ever would, there was no reason to stay. 'There's plenty of Galway folk in New York', says he, 'and you'll never miss a meal again.'

So, preparations were commenced to go to England to board one of the big ships that cross the Atlantic, as they didn't stop in Ireland.

Dada had been a hod carrier in the brick works in Galway City. I remember him as old and stooped over, with knotted hands and tight-lipped, the red brick dust imbedded in his pores. He seldom smiled and coughed all the time. He would be gone to the yard when we got up for school and I would bring him his lunch pail on my way to what he called the English School. He carried his hod of steaming bricks down the steep wooden ladder into the cooling room under ground and come up covered with sweat into the damp, chilly yard. Bill and Marty worked there only long enough to earn their passage to America. Marty said of the kilns, "I'll be in hell soon enough, no need to go for an interview every day." Bill urged, "We must get out from under the thumbs of the English landlords."

Once Frank and his pals joined H.M. Royal Irish Volunteers, sort of a National Guard, for the shilling a month, says Frank. "The uniform" says Bill "is better than honey." Frank had bought sweet cakes and we were having a grand old time when dada came in from the brickyard. He takes one look at Frank in the red uniform, marches to the mantelpiece, takes down his shillelagh and comes over and opens Frank's head, the blood running down onto the front of the new tunic. Dada says, "There'll be no red coats in this house while I'm out of my grave!" Frank and the Volunteers parted.

Dada was forty-six when he died, leaving mother with one pound, four and six, and two mouths to feed. Even the two pennies on his eyes were kept track of.

The night before we left, my best friend Mickey Barrett and I said our good-byes at the small bridge that crossed the drainage ditch we used to play about that lay behind the workers cottages on King Street in Garth. We didn't know whether to act as if we were only going to Dublin on a visit or whether we would never see each other again as though someone had died. He gave me a thrush in a cage he'd made himself. A wood thrush it was, with an olive-brown back and a yellow belly.

Mickey said, "They like a worm or a bit of fruit, you know."

I frowned, "I don't think they'll have worms on the boat."

"Well a nice fat spider, then."

"Aye. And a bit of wet biscuit, too, they favor."

"Keep it out of sight, goin' on the boat. I hear they don't allow no birds."

"How silly they are," says I, "As if the bird couldn't fly to America for free if it had a mind to."

"Remember the time we found the bottle of wine out behind the pub?"

"God, all I remember was waking up over my mother's shoulder, swaying back and forth. And all the neighbors laughing down the lane. I liked to die."

"Me, too. I was sick for a week. The two of us stretched out in this ditch."

In our bare feet, we kicked at tufts of grass, laughing at ourselves and the foolish rules of the English. Finally the silence grew solemn, we shook hands. I vowed to write him from America, telling of all the wonders we knew I would see.

Early the next morning, with the dew still on the thatched roofs, Mother, Jimmy and I loaded our few small bundles on Paddy Ryan's cart. Mother took down the crucifix that had always hung inside the front door, kissing it and slipped it into her knitting bag. She took one last look around the small room, the dirt floor, turf fire now dead for the first time in living memory. Silently, she closed the old faded plank door, which had never seen lock nor key.

"Well," says mother with a sigh, "Into the cart with you two."

We tried to conceal our anxiety for her sake. Of course, we didn't carry all the memories she did; who had lived in the cottage and who had died there.

Paddy helped mother up onto the front seat and taking the reins, says, "Will we go by the churchyard, missus, for old times sake?"

With one hand clutching the shawleen at her throat, she says, "Drive straight to the station." And turning to Jimmy and me sitting on the bundles in our Sunday best, "And you two, you keep them shoes on till we're on that boat."

My brothers and I had many times seen the trains come and go into the big stone station in Galway City; but of course had never been on one. Jimmy and I held our noses pressed to the window glass all the way to Dublin. The countryside that seemed to rattle by grew green and beautiful as we swayed through County Westmeath and County Kildare. Why was Galway, I wondered, all sand and rock and bog? We ate apples and biscuits mother had brung.

At Dublin, we walked from the train to the dock and crowded aboard a wooden paddle wheeler, where we were pressed together on long wooden benches. We dozed through the night, plowing across the Irish Sea to Liverpool.

Liverpool was long lines, tickets, passports, health certificates, all under big, shadowy, drafty tin sheds. Pat had sent mother receipts for the passage, which he had paid for in New York, along with a letter of instructions hard learned by him and the others. Jimmy and I stood awe-struck as waves of people flowed back and forth before us; soldiers with rifles and packs, sailors with round flat hats, one with a beautiful yellow and white bird on his shoulder, porters pushing baggage carts to and fro, men and women with trays, selling cakes and candy and apples. One had a sign on his box, "Prevent Mal de Mare 3d.". Jimmy and I looked at each other with open mouths and arched brows.

"Pay attention, you two", mother was saying. We looked at our coats to see men tying manila tags to our buttonholes. Mother said, "Now lads, they separate the men from the women on these boats."

"What for", I ask?

"To keep peace, they say," says she, looking annoyed at the English Customs Guard.

We were marched along on either side of a picket fence towards the boat. The boat, made of iron, was so high that we could not see the top of it.

Mother says to me over the fence, "Martin, you look after Jimmy, now." Jimmy commenced to cry.

Mother said, "Hush up! You make a show of me." Her eyes glistened as we all shuffled towards the big black ship.

I put my arm around Jimmy's shoulder and both shook him and drew him close to me. Clutching his shawl bundle to his chest in his cut down suit from one of the brothers, he was little more than a bundle of feathers quivering with fright and the tears held back, choking, big brown eyes with the long lashes and the little freckles scattered over the pale hollow cheeks.

Hidden under another shawl, I cradled my thrush in its small wicker cage. The wee bird was, I'm sure, too frightened to whistle and give us away.

Once up the gangplank and into the bowels of the ship, we were assigned to a bunk, only one being for the both of us because of our age someone said. The bunk was canvas stretched across a wooden frame. There were no blankets. The bunks were three high. Jimmy and I were on the bottom. We crawled into our bunk and observed as everyone settled into his new home, as it were.

Across from us, two young men went about laying out blankets and stowing their satchels for pillows, as though they had been on a ship before. One of them would leave and return to the bunks. Then the other would go away. Never were their possessions left unguarded. Jimmy and I adopted this caution.

A wee man with a moustache and eyeglasses, calling himself the Purser, came into our cabin where there were maybe thirty men and drew everyone's attention to the rules, posted on a wall. Then he began calling off everyone's name. When he said "Brown!" the man across from us who was to occupy the middle bunk, said "Aye." When he called out "Smith!" the other one in the lower bunk said, "Oh, aye, your worship." There was some laughter. When he saw I was looking at him, he winked. He was not too tall and had broad shoulders. He had black curly hair on top and hardly any on the sides. His twinkling eyes were dark brown under bushy black eyebrows. His face was weathered but not his neck. His nose had a little bend in it as though it had been broken. When he smiled, I saw a gap on one side of his teeth where a tooth was missing. The other one, Brown never smiled. He was forever mumbling under his breath and if he caught you looking at him, one of his eyes began to twitch. The first time, he curled up a fist at me and said, "And what are you gawking at, you little Irish bastard?"

Smith let off brushing a boot and says sweetly, "Easy with them hands, mate. That's why we're here ain't it though me darling?" And turning to me, Smith says, "Don't mind him, lad. Against Queen's Regulations for a Yorkshire man to be friendly."

We were well out to sea now and when the purser had gone, I uncovered the thrush to sea how he had fared. He fluttered about a bit at the light. Then he tweet-tweeted cautiously. I gave him a bit of biscuit and a drop of water in his little cup. The little brown thing preened himself, fluttering his wings as though clearing his pipes and began singing. His delicate notes went floating around the cabin. Smith turned from rummaging in a pack and said, "Ah, lad. That's a sweet thing you have there, a thrush. The pipes of an angel for sure." Some other men gathered round to listen and complimented Jimmy and me. Everyone began acting friendly and some men began whistling along with the bird. Jimmy was smiling, "Maybe we'll have some fun, Martin," says he.

We were given only breakfast and supper on the boat. Breakfast was always porridge and tea.

Supper was boiled potatoes or turnips and cabbage. There was no salt but Smith had some in his pocket, which he shared with Jimmy and me. On the third night, I recall, they gave us an apple. During the day we would go up on deck and see mother. She made friends, people leaving off their shyness when they saw we were all in the same condition. Jimmy and I spent many hours exploring the ship.

The rolling seas were boundless and when the days were cloudy, they were forbidding. To stem our awe of the vast uncertain gray-green force, which I think we all felt, Jimmy and I would concentrate on the structure of the ship and the crew who seemed to be able to look at the sea as we would on a field of hay and see things of comfort. Sometimes we would hang over the rail watching the sea passing by, rising and falling like a giant breast. This could be mesmerizing like a good turf fire, but when you looked at where the sea met the sky, at the silver-gray line that ran around your world endlessly, it was depressing. We saw seagulls and were sure land was near. Jimmy and I would run around the ship along side the railing looking for land. We never saw a speck. Later we were to learn that the seagulls ate the ship's garbage and slept on the stern at night. After a day of this and running up and down ladders, we slept like babes at night.

One man in our cabin would play softly on a concertina after supper. A boy played a tin whistle, its clear, delicate notes floating across the room as the men sucked on their little pipes, thinking, sometimes of home with its good and bad memories, and of the uncertainties of America. As long as Jimmy and I saw mother each day and got some grub, life was still an adventure. Once, she gave us each a toffee she'd gotten from a woman to whom she'd shown a new stitch. For them that had yarn the needles were always clacking for something to do, being kept away from their cooking and kettles, like fish from the water.

One white bearded old man in our cabin never left his bunk and men would bring him food and try to make him eat something. He would only take water. After seven or eight days, I awoke one morning to see bareheaded men carrying him out of the cabin. One said, "Ah well, old Seamus never did want to go to America." And another, "And no priest on this damn boat, neither."

Mister Smith had told us to call him, Smitty. He would squeeze a large index finger through the wooden bars of the cage and stroke the thrush ever so gently. He went about whistling a tune under his breath and always straightening his blanket or wiping his boots with a piece of rag. His clothes and Mister Brown's were worn and patched like an old man's but their boots were sturdy and well cared for. They had metal strips on the heels to keep them from wearing out.

Mister Brown was taller than Smitty. He had watery eyes and a red nose. His hair was reddish and very sparse on top. Red and blue veins were scattered across his flat, sallow cheeks. Smitty called him, Sandy. Brown would yell at us to cover the cage to stop the thrush's singing when he wanted to sleep in the afternoon. He had a bottle that he pulled at when he thought no on was watching. Once, when Smitty was away on deck, Sandy leaned out of his bunk with his red eyes and whispers to us in our bunk, "For thrupence, I'd chuck you two and that bird over the side." We quickly covered the cage. In a few minutes, Sandy was snoring loudly like dada of a Saturday night home from the pub.

166

One day, Smitty spoke to us in Gaelic. We only understood half of what he said. "Where are you from, lads, the West?"

"Galway." says I.

"Ah, beautiful Galway by the sea." says he.

"We get beat if we speak Gaelic in school."

"And beat at home if you speak English?" laughed Smitty.

"Aye." says Jimmy and I, grinning. I vaguely remember my grandfather sitting by the turf fire with his jug, singing the old Irish ditties. When he got drunk, you couldn't speak English around him or he'd whack you with his thorn stick. But there were very few that could carry on a conversation in Gaelic, only the curses and the blessings in the old tongue.

One stormy night, near the end of the voyage, as we were turning in, I said to Smitty, "Was you in the army?"

Smitty stopped brushing his boot. His eyes burned into mine and his face went dark. Sandy slid off his bunk and crouched next to us, looking from Smitty to me and back again. Jimmy was already asleep, as was the rest of the shadowy cabin. Me heart was in me mouth. I had struck a nerve, as they say. Sandy was breathing heavy and clutching and unclutching his big hands. I was wishing my brothers was near, I can tell you. Then the light came back into Smitty's face, "Now calm down, mate. Calm down. You're all nerves, me boy."

Sandy wiped the sweat from his brow, "You had to be so friendly and all with these two."

Smitty said, smiling at me, "And what makes you ask that, Martin me lad?"

Me brother," my voice shaking, says I, "was in the Volunteers. He had boots like yours." We all studied the boot in Smitty's hands. "But dada made him quit. 'Treason,' says he."

Smitty laughed, "And right he was, too, Martin. No good Irishman would put on a red coat unless he was got drunk first, eh, lads?"

Sandy turned his wrath against Smitty, "Speak for yourself, Paddy." says he, "There's other reasons for joining the bloody army."

"Yes." says Smitty, "And other reasons for quitting it, too."

Sandy whispered to Smitty, "I say we do them now with the blankets. This ship is the same as British soil. They could hang us here as well as in the Barracks Square."

"And we would deserve it. But not these two."

Sandy reached into his coat pocket and then so did Smitty.

"Oh, fuck off, Doyle." says Sandy, standing up. "He'll blab, I'm telling you." and groping his way to the cabin door, trips his way out into the passageway.

Smitty and I sat on our bunks in silence for a bit, listening to the soft chorus of breathing around us and the groaning of the ship as she rolled and plunged through the endless troughs of the dark Atlantic.

"I'm sorry to cause trouble." says I, feeling the tension I had set in motion and wishing I was back home.

"Sure it's not your fault, lad. He's the nervous sort, that Sandy."

"He's not Irish, is he?" says I for no good reason.

"No. English. No sense of humor at all, at all."

Smitty was thoughtful for awhile, then he says, "Martin. Can you keep a secret?"

"Aye." says I, bending closer.

"You see, it's like this. Sandy and me was in the British Army and we got into a scrap in front of a pub with a sergeant. Sergeants are always belligerent, don't you know. But this one had a skull like an eggshell. Sandy knocked him down and he never got up. Them English cities with their granite curbstones."

"Oh." says I.

"An accident to be sure, Martin. But still, it would have been the rope for both of us." Smitty craned his neck inside of his tattered shirt.

"I'll say nothin'." says I.

"There's the good lad. Poor Sandy, though, with his drinking, he sees a Provost Marshall behind every tree, or every bunk, as it were. He'll bear watching 'till I get him off this boat."

"Should I go tell him everything's all right?" I stood up to go and show my good faith to Sandy.

Smitty took hold of my coat, "No." says he, "You stay with your brother. And don't let yourself be found out on deck alone with Sandy, either. He's not in his best humor these days, don't you know."

"Oh, yes." says I, not really understanding it all.

Smitty stood up. "I know where he's to be found. I'll go and reassure him everything's all right. You go to bed and I'll see you in a wee bit" says he, winking at me.

I crawled into my bunk, under the shawl next to Jimmy. Smitty rummaged in his pack for a moment and then silently went out of the cabin door.

When I awoke the next morning, it was under a big warm blanket. Then we were all up and pulling on our boots. Smitty looked like he had been up all night, maybe playing cards.

I said, "Where's Sandy?" His bunk was bare. His satchel and blankets were gone. Then I saw that the blanket that had lain over Jimmy and me was one of Sandy's

Smitty said, "He's found new mates down the other end of the ship." Smitty's twinkling eyes held mine.

Jimmy said "I'm hungry."

Smitty went on, "They're all English. Sandy'll bunk with them. He's took his gear. He left that blanket for you and Jimmy. You can have his bunk, Martin."

"Thanks." says I. There was a silence between us.

Smitty reached down and took the cover off the thrush. It began warbling away. There's a grand sound," says he, "Something to remind of us of home in a foreign land, eh, Martin?"

"Aye," says I, "A foreign land".

Two mornings more and the big rusty links of the anchor chain tumbled, rattling out of the bow chocks, plunging beneath the calm waters of a new harbour in a new land on a bright new morning. A warm breeze carried the smells of paint and tar, and grass and trees, and bakeries and fish to us. The New York shore was a forest of black and white masts sparkling in the morning sunshine, as well as smokestacks. Seagulls wheeled, screeching overhead. Tugboats chugged to and fro. Small white sailed cutters and sloops darted through the water, each flying the colorful flags of the different steamship companies.

Martin never saw Smitty nor Sandy again.

And that's how my grandfather came to America.

THE PERSONAL TOUCH

Ever befuddled Chester Entwhistle stumbled from the old courthouse waving his validated petition allowing him to run, yet again, for town selectman, a post he has been chasing for ten years. His core supporters were on hand to kick-off his campaign; his mother and his dog, Tom, named after Chester's idol, Thomas Jefferson. The whittling wits of the courthouse steps were on hand to guffaw our own political Don Quixote in his fifth bid for public office.

Town Selectman didn't pay but $2,000 per annum. There were three of them. All they did was appoint the Dog Warden, the Traffic Warden and the Town Librarian. But it must be remembered that Selectman was the first stepping stone for many a prominent personage in our fair state. Why, even the current governor was once a humble selectman. Of course, back then you didn't need a high school diploma.

One selectman was elected each year for two years. Thus ensuring their overlapping terms would ease the transmission of the vast storehouse of know-how built up over the years by the sages who had occupied the august post, also it discouraged coups, kind of like the Senate but without the free haircuts and snuff.

Now Chester was well qualified for the post: steeped in the works of J.J. Rousseau, Edmund Burke, Tom Paine and Thomas Jefferson. He had a keen grasp of the principles and practices of democracy. But Chester couldn't always put a name to the many faces he greeted in front of the post office on a Saturday morning. This pricked many a vanity, but folks generally liked to see it as scatterbrained on Chester's part.

171

Chester's opponent on this occasion was young Rexford 'Rex' Braun. Rex had been the high school quarterback and BMOC, (big man on campus). Girls called him the 'profile'. Rex's father owned three car dealerships, but Rex said he wanted to start at the bottom, and he did, as an associate in the stock department of KallMarts. They let Rex go after the sports equipment inventory went wide of receipts. Later that season, Rex was seen trying to pass off a gross of sports bras as double thick athletic supports.

Rex drew a blank with Edmund Burke and Tom Paine. He was sure The Rights of Man was a heavy metal group and that Rousseau was the second-string goalie for the Oilers. Rex had once seen a documentary on Paris, (unable to locate his remote), and was amazed to learn that even the children spoke French 'like a native'. But to be fair, Rex did possess those all-important qualities found in all successful clergymen, used car salesmen and politicos: a killer smile and he never forgot a name! Meanwhile, Chester was never easy with people, especially at blowing his own horn, an instrument at which Rex excelled.

On a crisp but mild election eve, Chester was restless and left campaign headquarters, his mother's kitchen, for a last walk down Main Street. Maybe he would run into a few undecideds whose names he might mercifully remember.

Chester was startled when his old high school science teacher, Professor Van Vinkle stepped out of the shadows of a giant sycamore. Upon receiving his doctorate the professor had secured a post at the state university teaching electro-spectro magnetism, (Don't ask me.). He was the designer of the new octagon scalometer just installed in the physics department to much fanfare within the scientific community. You may have read something of it at the dentist's. Professor Van Vinkle always had a soft spot in his heart for Chester, a fellow maladroit.

"Professor, did you come home to vote?"

"Nein! I never vote. It only encourages the wrong types. But I came to see you my boy! How is your lovely mother?"

"Fine. I'm running for Selectman in tomorrow's election."

"I know, I know. That's why I'm here. Your opponent is a grinning buffoon with the depth of a shadow. Most voters prefer a candidate they can look down on so they can hold him to the same low standards to which they hold themselves. Thus, 'All Braun and no brains' is a shoo-in."

"I don't stand a snowball's chance."

"Have no fear. Van Vinkle is here! Come with me. I have my old van with me, half home away from home, and half laboratory. I may be able turn the election over."

"Around?"

"Whatever."

As they passed under a streetlight, Chester noticed that the professor still wore the same old, baggy, chalk stained sports coat he wore in the classroom. Chester hadn't seen the professor in several years, and apparently neither had his barber.

"So, how's things at the university, Professor?"

"Ach! Don't ask. They want to take away my tenure. All for one chemistry lab wall. They have three left. It let in much needed light. A metaphor. The shortsighted fools."

The professor led Chester down a dark side street and into his large van, which bristled with aerials. Once inside, he thrust Chester into what looked like a reclaimed barber's chair, lowered an elaborate

173

headset onto Chester's head, and stuffed a list of names and addresses into the nervous young man's hands.

"What's this?"

"This is a list I have compiled of voters who traditionally never vote. They comprise thirty-five percent of the eligible voters in this town."

"What good is this? Where did you get it?"

"Does Macy's tell Gimble's? Don't ask. Listen, those who regularly vote, vote straight party ticket. You won't sway them at the last minute. But those who don't vote, we don't know what they're thinking, if at all! Relax. You will schmooze. You'll commiserate."

"But there must be over a hundred names here. How could I visit a hundred voters at this late hour?"

The professor continued with his preparations, plugging in electrical wires to the headset, "Look at the first name. Read it."

Chester peered at the list, "George and Esther Amstel, Deeks Road, off Route 145."

"You know them?"

"Sure. George is a semi-retired dairyman. Etti still puts up her own preserves. See them on Saturdays when they come into town. Etti donates her preserves to the church bazaar."

"Yes, yes, very folksy. Pepper of the earth, I'm sure. Sit back. I have to strap you in. This is still experimental. Chester, you have your will made out? Relax. It's a joke."

"Is this going to be like a virtual reality thing?"

"Even more better. You will drive up to the Amstel ranch. Get out, sit on the porch, and listen. Listen more than talk. You'll say, more than they should vote for you, they should just vote. It's something if

174

they give it up, it don't come back so easy. And don't worry; you won't forget a name, either. Ready?"

· "What do I have to lose?"

The professor began flipping switches, pulling levers, pushing rheostats. Lights winked, fluorescent tubes fluttered into life, pulsating. Chester's Medusa-like helmet hummed and began to steam a little – or was it smoke?

Chester believed he was in his car tooling down Route 145. The professor was searching his vest pockets for a cigarette butt. Yes, yes, he would quit tomorrow for sure.

George Amstel sat on his front porch with his Aussy-shep, Dot. It was a warm evening and the air was sweet with the turning of the leaves and wood smoke drifting off into the pine stand above the house.

Chester honked as he approached, and Etti came out drying her hands. She smiled and waved him up onto the porch. She was a friendly, lively woman, the opposite of George. This is sometimes called balance.

George said, "You're welcome to sit, but don't waste your breath about voting."

"Oh, hush up. It's only Chester. Beer? Lemonade?"

"Lemonade sounds good, ma'am. How's everyone been?"

Black and white Dot padded over, gave Chester the once over and returned to her spot next to George's bench. Etti busied herself culling a sack of potatoes, casting away the mushy ones. They talked of road repair and school busses.

Eventually, George voiced his complaints: the politicians spent all their time getting re-elected and raising money for TV. What time did they spend on the needs of the people?

Chester said – and he wasn't sure where it came from – "You know, Mister Amstel, you may be right. But I have to tell you this: Many of the people, who do vote regularly, rich and poor alike, don't really want you to vote. 'Cause if you did, their vote would count for less."

"How so?"

"Let's say there are a hundred eligible voters in a town and only twenty-five vote. Their vote carries the weight of four. You're giving them your voting power but still paying your share of the taxes. They get to say how and by whom your tax dollars are spent. They're glad you stay home. This way the politicians only have to answer to a small group of taxpayers while getting to spend the taxes of all. But if you're happy sitting on your porch while Amos Duncan has your say…"

"Amos claims he never votes."

"When you find a good fishing hole, do you go shouting it all over the county?"

"Damn them all!", George stomped into the kitchen, slamming the screen door.

Etti followed Chester to his car, thrusting a Pyrex covered pie at him, "I swear I can see your ribs, Chester."

"Too bad you're not registered, Etti."

"Oh, we're registered, all right. I send in the absentee ballots every year. Sort of keeping up our membership."

"You sign George's name?"

"I won the penmanship medal three years running in Central School."

It went much like that for the rest of Chester's journey. He'd stop before going up a hill road and

176

look at the next name on the list, recalling when he'd seen them last, who all their kin were, and how best to appeal to their better natures, what would enlighten their self-interest.

When the professor raised the headset, Chester was perspiring.

"Wow! I'm bushed. But I never forgot a name, from Amstel to Zoicher. How long was I gone?"

"Maybe five minutes. Chester, do you by any chance have a cigarette?"

The next day the turnout was the highest since FDR ran in 1936. Chester won two-to-one. The State Ledger sent a reporter down from the capital to interview the victor. They had a good laugh down at the barbershop when Rex demanded a recount. (Chester, now Chess to everyone, went on to the State Assembly and then the State Senate).

At the victory party, pizza and adult beverages over at the Calico Café, Chester confided a guilty feeling to the professor.

Professor Van Vinkle summed up, "Listen, my boy, it's like years ago, the first candidate to stand on a tailgate instead of a tree stump to campaign, the first to let his fingers do the walking and use the phone, the first to use radio, TV to reach the voters. So, you were the first to use the hologram. It's not illegal."

"But I still feel a little uneasy."

"Look, sometimes virtue needs a hand-up."

"Leg-up."

"Whatever. Got a cigarette?"

Compassionate Leave

During the late spring of 1953 the Marines listened to the news of the peace talks at Panmunjom on the radio with one ear and with the other for the 'ping' of barbed wire being cut in front of them in the night.

Vincent Mannion awoke with a start around midmorning in his bunker. He drank half a canteen cup full of water and had a cigarette. Lemmuel, the beady-eyed rat who shared the bunker with them pressed against a sandbag above a 12x12 roof beam watching Vincent whose rising had interrupted his morning chow run. Vincent found a lint covered soda cracker in his breast pocket and tossed it into a corner where after a decent interval; Lemmuel darted over and retrieved it, disappearing again between the sandbags. It was then that Vincent saw the letter propped against a c-ration can on the little oil stove they used for heat and to heat their chow on. Somebody must have dropped it off while he was sleeping. The only time he could really rest was when the sun was comfortably up. He sat there for a while staring at the clean white envelope as yet uncontaminated by the all pervasive mud and sandy grit of Korea. He hadn't received a letter for over four months, not since he had written Bernadette to tell her to stop writing. Her chatty, silly letters which had been such fun in Parris Island had become obscene against the buff colored manila tags the corpsmen tied to buttonholes of our glorious dead and names axed off company rosters by company clerks. His original squad of thirteen was now down to eight. Mapleleaf and Maloney who had shared this bunker with him for eleven months were gone, both out to the hospital ship, Mapleleaf all shot up and Maloney in a reefer waiting for poncho rotation. Only two weeks before they had been caught in a probing barrage while returning with a chigee train from the O.P. Vincent had dived down one side of the dike while Mapleleaf and Maloney had scrambled down the other side and had both gotten hit. There would be no replacements until the next rotation draft dropped anchor at Inchon in a week or so.

The envelope was written in his sister Maureen's handwriting. Being Irish, Vincent had learned to assume that most letters bore bad news. It was from his father but in Maureen's hand. His mother was dying. They had put off telling him at her insistence. She had been sure of a remission. Vincent heard the phrase, 'remission of sins.' She slipped in and out of a coma, asking for Vincent, her baby. She had two weeks at best. Could he possibly come home? He had been gone from Garnet Street for twenty-one months. He never missed the filthy tenement a moment, with its railroad flats, no central heating, where they froze in winter around a kerosene stove and baked in summer amid the rising odors of coffee grounds and orange peels drifting up from the uncovered garbage cans outside the front door, mingled with the Lysol his mother used on the hall linoleum to mask the cat spray.

Vincent took the letter to the Platoon Sergeant, who took him to the First Sergeant. The First Sergeant spoke to the Captain. The Captain said he'd see what he could do. The next day the company clerk ran up to him to say the First Sergeant wanted to see him. The First Sergeant told him to turn in his rifle, flak jacket, helmet and web gear to the supply sergeant, pack his sea bag and hightail it over to Battalion where the papers were waiting. He had been granted a Compassionate Leave. From

Battalion he hitched a ride on a truck to Ascom City, the repo depot for the First Division where he picked up his other sea bag with his dress uniforms, thence to Kimpo Airport where he changed into khakis and hitched a ride on a C-130 Flying Boxcar to Kyoto where he stayed overnight at an R and R camp. The next day he got a hop to Hawaii on a DC-4 MATS airliner with a lot of brass. He was the only enlisted man he saw. The stewardess made a fuss over him. "What are those little stars on the blue ribbon for?" One for each three months in combat, he said. The army major sitting in the window seat with the briefcase open before him was looking out the window pretending he hadn't heard. He had four rows of ribbons but no stars. The stewardess straightened up, "Well, we certainly don't see much of that on this flight, sugar. Now you just wave if there's anything you want." She knew Vincent had come from some place not nice; while his face was tanned, his forehead above his dark eyebrows was pale where it was always covered by his helmet. His hands were scratched and his nails dirty. He loosened his tie and lay back in the soft seat. The last time he was in a seat this comfortable was at the dentist's.

Vincent tossed and turned, the theme of his thoughts was that his relationship with his father had changed and that the old man had better accept it if they were to get along. Korea had changed him. He had always been afraid of needles, injections. He died a thousand deaths on the day he was to be brought to the doctor's for an injection for this or that. In Parris Island they shuffled along in winding lines with their dungaree jackets tied around their waists, their tee shirt sleeves rolled up. They entered a long Quonset hut. A row of corpsmen on either side stood

180

behind small porcelain tables with trays of syringes, alcohol and swabs. Were the corpsmen leering? All his eighteen years of accumulated cowardice welled up inside him. All the bravado of moments ago dried up. They had brought into the hut the smell of young sweat, new dungarees and new leather boondockers but it was overcome by the alcohol and the heat of a crowded hut in summer. Somewhere up ahead a corpsman said loudly, "Don't tense up, boy. You'll only make it worse!" The long row ahead of Vincent shuffled silently through the gauntlet. He stepped up to the first corpsman who didn't even look at him. Vincent thought of the men who had gone before him; they're no better than me. And his fear left him. They were rushed through so quickly that one corpsman had pulled away the syringe without the needle. Vincent took out the needle and tossed it on the next tray. Once outside, the guy in front of him stiffened up and went over into the sand. Will I be the same, he thought, tough it through for only a little while? He didn't faint. He felt good. It was only a little thing he knew but it would come to help him later on when involuntary bowel movements were predicted. It was a whole string of nameless little victories that had brought him to this point. He was hardly a year older, no grey hairs, no wrinkles but he was changed. He started to drift off. He was afraid the first time in a plane. Now he didn't give a shit if this one crashed. He knew life was a day-to-day operation, that clocks and calendars were only records of the past and wishful thinking. Vincent had fallen asleep to the drone of the DC-4's four engines and been awakened by first light as they flew eastward. Someone had covered him with an airline blanket during the night. The major tossed uncomfortably next to him, his mouth open, no blanket.

At the Military Air Transport Command terminal of Honolulu Airport, Vincent was directed to a section set aside for servicemen looking for hops, free rides on military aircraft if there was an empty seat. Vincent could never have afforded a commercial flight. An army captain examined and stamped his leave papers. He assigned Vincent a number and told him to listen for his name and number to be called out over the P.A. system for the next hop to L. A. Enlisted men sat and lay sprawled over heavy leather and chrome couches, smoking, playing cards, drinking cokes, sleeping, reading newspapers and comic books. Vincent sat on his sea bag in a corner smoking a cigarette. He had never seen such a salty bunch before. They were all Chiefs, Master Sergeants and Tech Sergeants with enough hash marks between them to stretch the length of a chow line. Vincent didn't see anyone less than a staff sergeant. There were many reasons for their presence. Some were being transferred to Embassy Duty, some taking a shipping over leave, some experts in torpedo gyroscopes badly needed on some sub in San Diego, some were drivers for Generals or Admirals, some were instructors in scuba, demolitions or radar, maybe even the favorite cook or baker of some Division Commander. But Compassionate Leave was rare at that time.

Vincent looked over at the counter to see the major who had sat next to him on the plane talking to the captain behind the counter. The captain handed his clipboard to the major who ran his eye up and down the list of names. He said something to the captain. The captain frowned, shaking his head from side to side. The major tapped the gold leaf on his shoulder and the captain shrugged and scratched off a name on the list. The major waved to him and sauntered out through the glass doors into the shimmering heat.

A short time later, Vincent heard his name and number being paged over the P.A. system. He went up to the counter. The captain said, "Sorry, Mannion. You got bumped. You're the lowest rank in the room. I'll try to get you on the next plane out. Probably this afternoon. Come back about 1300 hours. Here. Here's a meal chit. Here, take two. There's a restaurant in the main building. It's not bad. I'm sorry as hell about this. I told them it's a Compassionate Leave. Usually no one bumps a Compassionate Leave. That's the way the fucking military works. So, listen; leave your gear here behind the counter. I'll watch out for it. It's hot enough without it. If only Colonel Webber were here. He's out on the links. So, come back about 1300, OK? We'll see what we can do on the afternoon flight to L.A."

From L.A. International Vincent got a hop on a C-47 to El Toro. At El Toro he called his sister Maureen. She said, "Mama passed away last night at the hospital. Very peaceful. She had the priest and all. Father Collins. He was her favorite. She always went to him for confession. It was really a blessing, Vinnie. I'm wrung out. How have you been?"

"OK. I'm still going to try for a hop to Quantico. From there I can take the train to New York. So, how's pop? Barricaded in Degnan's I suppose!"

"No. He's been good. He was at Holy Family Hospital with me for the last three days. And when I had to take care of the baby he stayed there alone. Nothing to drink. He's been good. Of course that won't last."

Vincent got off the subway at his old stop, Van Broome and Second Street. When he came out of the entrance the first thing he saw was Degnan's Bar and Grill, Degnan's saloon. The boss, Joe Degnan always called it the 'store'. He ran a tight ship, no under-age drinkers. If you cursed or swore he'd throw you out and you'd be eighty-sixed for a week or ten days for the first offense. If you started a fight, a month. And Joe was not above cutting you off if he thought you'd had enough. Of course he was always Mister Degnan to the kids. His son, Joey who was taking over more and more of the load, like filling the ice box around the pipes and pounding it down with an old worn bat, was always after the old man to modernize the store since he came home from the war. He was always trying to get the customers and salesmen to call him Joe but he was always Joey or even Little Joey by the old timers, the trolley car drivers who hung out in the store since the electric busses replaced the trolleys. Many had refused to learn how to drive the busses and retreated from line to line as the routes were replaced by the electric busses until the last line in Brooklyn, McDonald Avenue was turned over to busses. It was in the papers, with pictures. The last old motorman with his handle standing in front of the trolley, the young bus driver in his new Ike jacket uniform standing next to the shiny new bus. Some said don't be sentimental for the trolleys but as old Mrs. Ryan would say, "At least the trolley would wait for you if they saw you running down the block with your packages and your heels hitting you in the arse."

It was about seven a.m. The store opened at eight, except on Sundays of course. The front and side doors were chocked open to air the place out. Across the two piece plate glass window in front were the faded gilded letters in an old Spenserian script, 'Degnan's Bar & Grill', and down in one corner like a business card, 'Ladies Entrance around the corner.' Degnan's faced north-east and was always in dark shadow in the mornings. Vincent peeked through the doorway. The floor was wet with C-N and water where Joey had just mopped. He was down the back with his back turned finishing the mopping. Vincent half expected to see his old man holding up his section of the bar, all the excuse in the world to get drunk as early as he could; but the store was empty. As bars went it was the cleanest. They cleaned the pipes every Thursday morning and if you were passing you could hear the pebbles flowing through the taps and hoses scraping away the scum that the flowing beer left in its wake. There were no curtains or blinds in the windows to hide behind. Only the very young and very old stood near the front window. Degnan's was for the brave and the honest. The once white, high tin ceiling with its old wooden bladed fans was fast moving from a yellow caramel to a sooty brown from years of tobacco smoke. He remembered seeing it painted in 1948 when they got their first TV in, to see Uncle Milty. Old Joe was dead against it like he was the bar stools. But the balance sheet dictated the change. "Bar stools bring women. And women bring trouble", Joe Degnan always said. The windows were washed every Monday, inside and out. Small potted palms sat on a sill inside the front window. There were no neon beer signs. Degnan's was as dignified as any bank or funeral parlor. But the younger guys were drifting away since V-J Day. They were all beginning to have cars and the married ones gone to Levittown and Staten Island. They would come back for a while for the soft ball games and the Annual Communion Breakfast in the spring, then only on Christmas, then they would stop coming. After four or five years the only time you saw all the guys that had been in World War II was for a wedding or a wake.

Vincent was in no hurry to go either home to see the old man in his underwear drinking his coffee with a shot in it or to Flood's Funeral Home, which didn't open until ten. Flood's consisted of one floor with two rooms, or parlors. If more than two people died within a four-day period; the third would have to be waked elsewhere. The office was right off the street, a roll-top desk and potted palms. A heavy purple curtain on a brass rod separated it from the first room.

To go directly home from Degnan's he'd have to pass Flood's. He went down Second Street and along Wyckoff Street, the back way to Garnet Street only two blocks from Degnan's. The way dad went from his job at Kretchmer's Bakery when he was banned from Degnan's. The way mom went to avoid Mike's grocery store when she was behind on the bill. The way Vincent went to avoid a fight. The way Maureen went to avoid her girlfriends when they had new Easter outfits, congregating outside of Bartel's Ice Cream Parlor on Sunday after Mass, and she hadn't one. As long as he didn't go to Flood's he could still see his mother sitting under the lamp in her favorite chair reading the Journal American. "Listen to this, will you!" she'd say and read out something from the paper. Maureen and he would be doing their homework at the dining room table. "And don't forget to throw back that cloth. I don't want any ink on that. That's one of my best." "Mom, why can't we do our homework in the kitchen?"

"Because I want you two scholars where I can see you, that's why."

Around the house, dad was always humming a tune if he was sober. As he took on more oil he began to sing, songs from Broadway or the latest record. Then he'd reach a point where he'd begin to get sloppy and melancholy, and the old Irish songs would come out. That's how Vincent learned "Toora loora loora". He had a pretty good voice and could really hit the high notes. "Listen to him, will you Helen. He's an Irish thrush, he is, he is.", dad would say, a tear in his eye. "He is that." mom would reply, both of them in the mock Irish brogue that they would never dare use in front of their immigrant parents. After he had started school in St. Theresa's and was old enough to be scraping his knees on his own along Van Broome Street with his pals, sometimes they'd be galloping down the street in front of Degnan's after school or on a Saturday morning and his father would dash out the front door and waylay him and bring him inside and stand him on the end of the bar and say to Joe Degnan, Look at the bird I just caught!" "What kind is it?" someone would say. "He looks like a thrush. Let's see can he sing. Will you give us a song, Vinnie, for a soda?" Vincent would be all red faced and stare down at the bar top. "Give us a song, Vinnie." one or two would shout. He'd look up at dad who'd say, "Toora loora', Vinnie." and wink. Once he began to sing the shyness left him. He'd just pick out an object on the back wall over all the heads and focus on it. On the last note he'd reach for the ceiling never imagining he couldn't reach the high note. When he'd finished, there wasn't a dry eye in the house. One of the few times you could get an Irishman to cry, after his pump was primed with beer or whiskey. Mister Degnan would give Vincent a small White Rock orange and he'd be chased out the door. There was always someone

187

there to help him drink the soda. Only after he was out on the street did he notice he was ringing wet with perspiration. There was no television then. Only the radio to listen to the ball games. He wasn't much of an interruption. This went on two or three times a year. After a while he was too tall to be stood on the bar and stood on a chair. It was during one of these times that he noticed his father had a bald spot. As he grew taller it grew wider. As he grew older, when he'd be hitting the high note at the end he'd catch sight of someone's face, anxious that he'd hit it. Vincent guessed they knew, as he didn't; that it was only a matter of time before his voice would crack like a wine glass that would no longer ring when you struck it. Before he realized what a gift he had, it was gone. A boy knows when his voice is gone before his father will admit to it. One day as he was going by the store, his father snagged him. Vincent tried to get away but dad was drunk and quick to dramatize everything. No more chair, Vincent was almost as tall as him. He wouldn't let go of his son's arm. "Give us a song, Vinnie." "Oh, leave the lad alone, Frank." Mister Degnan said, seeing how mortified he was. "I can't sing anymore, dad." "You can't sing anymore! He never shuts up around the house. Give us a song, Vinnie. Don't be stuck up." "I can't do it, dad." He tightened his grip on his arm and his grin got wider. Mister Degnan said, "Leave him, Frank. Can't you see his voice is changing?" "You won't even try?" "No." "Well get out of here then." he let go of Vincent's arm, pushing him away from him. As Vincent was leaving, his face crimson, his father said; "Oh, how sharper than a serpent's tooth is an ungrateful child."But Vincent could tell that everyone had already turned back to the Dodger game on the new television. That was the beginning of the rift between them.

As Vincent neared home he spotted the small bunch of flowers pinned to the front door post, white and yellow pom-poms of some sort, and the card from Flood's, "Helen Mary Mannion" in a fine if shaky script, black, black ink on the crisp white card. He tossed his sea bag behind the door to the cellar and left the dark hall, it smelling of cat piss masked with C-N, the beat up garbage cans reeking of rotting cabbage and leftovers gone bad, mixed with a pleasant scent of oranges and coffee grounds. He went down to the canal, still on a Saturday, its cranes and rusty buckets hanging mute above the sand barges. He sat on a bollard and stared at the still, purple and chartreuse substance that floated there.

On Saturday nights, dad would dress up to go to Degnan's. "Why bother?" They'd ask. "I may go on from there," he'd say, straightening his tie. Vincent and his mother would exchange smirks. He never got beyond Degnan's that they knew of. After Friday night's drunk in Degnan's dad slept most of Saturday. They tiptoed around him. When it came to those father and son things Vincent always said dad worked on Saturdays. Before television, Maureen and he would be glued to the radio listening to their favorite Saturday programs. Dad would knock off whatever beer was left in the house while he was dressing. Then he would get annoyed at them for listening to such trash and come over and change the station to classical music. He'd sit on the couch, conducting the orchestra with his beer glass for about fifteen minutes while lecturing them on improving their taste in music. Then he'd abruptly leave. The children would quickly turn back to their program but they'd have lost the thread of the story. He did this; it seemed to them, every Saturday night. Mom never said anything but Vincent could tell from the way she snapped and rattled her paper that she was annoyed, too. By the time he was ten, he had all but given up on the promises to be taken to the beach or to Ebbets Field. A child will make up a ton of excuses to surpress the hatred that slowly builds up. During Lent his father gave up the drink and they all half pretended he had reformed. They easily pretended they were a happy family out of a B-movie. Then he would become a stickler for homework and not staying out at night and how clean the house was. Holy Saturday afternoon when they took the purple covers off the statues in St. Theresa's and when Frank marched into Degnan's Helen and the kids breathed sighs of relief.

It was ten o'clock. Vincent could not bring himself to go to Flood's. Not alone. Nor did he want to see his father in his underwear, unshaven, his bald spot dominating, and the brown quart bottles of Ballantine's beer on the chipped porcelain kitchen table. He had a vision of himself down the road, sitting across the kitchen table from his father both of them hung over, each waiting for the other to make the coffee, Maureen long gone to the suburbs, a sink full of greasy dishes, and the refrigerator a biologist's dream of spore cultures. Who would murder whom first?

Avoiding the house he went back up to Van Broome Street. A lot of people were up and shopping. He ran into Mrs. Ryan trudging along in her slippers clutching her bag of empty beer bottles. She lived one floor below them. People who live that close in tenements pretend not to know each other's business and display a tolerance found less among single family dwellers. Mrs. Ryan was an older widow whom Helen Mannion would go to when she was younger for advice. Later, his mother would go to the stores for Mrs. Ryan when she was under the weather in the winter. She was shocked to see the young Marine. "Vincent! My God, you're home. When did you get home? It was a mercy but I don't know what we're going to do around here without your mother. Have you been home, yet?"

"Yes." he lied.

"Well, then you know the worst. Little lamby, I'm so sorry. Did you see Maureen? I saw her yesterday at Flood's. The baby's gotten so big! And I see she's due again. Maybe it'll be a girl this time. Well, I have to get my dress out of the cleaners. I'll see you in Flood's then?"

"Yes", he said. When you wanted to, with Mrs. Ryan, you could be silent and no one noticed. She could hold up both ends of the conversation with ease.

Passing Degnan's again, he looked in. Mister Degnan was behind the stick and Joey was still doing the floors in back. Mr. Degnan saw him and waved him in, coming around the bar. He had a suit jacket in his hand. He shook Vincent's hand, "Sorry for your troubles, Vincent."

"Thank you, Mr. Degnan."

"This is your father's coat. Better take it home. Might need it. He was in here just two nights ago. It was a warm night and I guess he forgot his coat."

"He'd forget his head...mom used to say."

"A wonderful woman, your mother. A saint."

Joey piped up from the back, "Vinnie, they let you come home? You couldn't get a leave in World War Two. They wouldn't let you come home if your mother..."

Mister Degnan cleared his throat and interrupted, "Joey, will we leave off with your memoirs for now? Are you not finished yet?"

Joey stood up from leaning on his mop, "Sorry for your troubles, Vinnie."

"Will you have something, Vincent?"

"No, thanks. I better get up to the house."

"Well, we'll see you later on then, up at Flood's"

Vincent decided he couldn't stall any longer and began walking towards the house. He remembered a pin he gave his mother for Christmas when he was fifteen. He was delivering groceries for Roualston's. The pin was made up of three paste emeralds in the shape of a shamrock. She wore it to bingo once and won, and wore it to bingo ever after. Her lucky pin, she called it. Frank gave her a pin that same Christmas with some seed pearls. When she would be dressing to go out other than to bingo Vincent would watch to see which pin she'd wear. She always wore the pearl. "Why?" he'd say. "The shamrock doesn't always go, Vinnie. Don't be in a mood." She'd say, "You're my best beau, Vinnie. And that's the God's honest truth." She'd kiss him on the way out the door, leaving a trail of Lily-of-the-valley behind her.

When he reached the house and the funeral bouquet above the garbage cans, there was a baby carriage next to the railing. He guessed it was Maureen's boy whom he'd never seen. He was sleeping. There were fine particles of soot on his little white face. They came from the giant smoke stacks of the gas works a few blocks away. You learned to ignore the soot on the sheets taken in off the line but didn't expect to see it on a baby's new face, a fighting chance at least! He picked up the sea bag and slung it easily onto his shoulder with one hand. In boot camp he had trouble lifting it and couldn't manage to balance it for a long time.

He went up the dark staircase, the steps creaking beneath him. When he reached the landing beneath his Maureen came out onto the landing, "Vinnie?"

"Maureen?"

She wore a corduroy maternity jumper and ran down the stairs to greet him. She hugged and kissed him. His hands were full and he didn't have to respond. They had never been much for kissing in their family. "Did you see your nephew? Did you see the baby? Little Philip."

"Yeah. He's beautiful."

Maureen began to wail and wring her hands, "Oh, Vinnie, it's a nightmare. It's terrible."

"Yeah. I tried. I tried to get here on time. Some bastard of an army major bumped me in Hawaii."

"Daddy's dead."

"I must have been on six different air planes. I was on a transcontinental from Japan to Honolulu, a flying boxcar from Korea to Japan. A D-C6 to El Toro in California.

What?"

"Daddy's dead, too. He died yesterday morning. It's a nightmare around here."

He looked at the apartment door, "Where is he?"

"At Flood's. They're both there at Flood's."

He climbed onto the landing and dropped the sea bag, holding onto his father's jacket.

Mrs. Ryan appeared at the foot of the landing in dress, hat and gloves, "Maureen? Vinnie?"

"He didn't know about daddy." Maureen sniveled, "He just found out."

"All right, all right!" he said, trying to take it all in.

Vincent thought when guys you were close to in Korea got suddenly killed you backed away from them, telling yourself you were not really that close to them. You and the guy who told you both stared at the ground. You'd ask if there was any hot coffee around. You'd look through the hill of C-ration boxes looking for grapefruit sections, the only thing that seemed to relieve the dryness in your throat. Later when you were alone you cursed your cowardice. But it didn't go away.

"I don't understand? How could this happen? Things like this don't happen. Not two at once."

Mrs. Ryan wiped her nose with a good handkerchief, "Oh, Vincent, I thought you knew."

"It happened right here on the stairs. Yesterday morning. Daddy and me were in Flood's, you know, just before they open to see mama looked o.k. and all. We have her in that nice blue dress she liked, her favorite. And daddy says, "The pin, the pin, that's what it needs. I'll run up and get that pin.""

"You know the pin you gave her. The shamrock one. Mr. Flood and me are waiting and waiting. Where is he? I almost went down to Degnan's to look. Then Philly runs in, 'Your father collapsed in the house. They took him away in the ambulance to Holy Family."

"Where is Philly?"

"Oh, in Degnan's I suppose, where else? He can't take any pressure, that one."

Mrs. Ryan had come up the stairs, "I was getting ready to go out to the stores when I heard someone running up the stairs. I thought it was one of the kids. I looked out to give them a piece of my mind and I see Frank half way up these stairs. And then, boom! He falls down, clutching his chest. I says 'Frank! Frank! What is it? He had no color in his face at all. I ran down to Mrs. Doyle's. She's the nearest phone.

Her husband's a fireman, so he goes to the head of the list for the phones. She called the ambulance."

Maureen said, "The police said he was dead on arrival, massive heart attack."

"But he was never sick."

"Not a day." said Mrs. Ryan.

"Did he say anything before they took him away?" Vincent asked.

"Oh, he just kept saying, 'Helen, Helen', you know like."

"I never got to see him." Maureen said, her hands to her cheeks, staring off into the shadows.

He stood on the landing, his hands gripping the railing, staring down into the shadows of the stairwell. Mrs. Ryan said, "Now you two take hold. I'll see you over at Flood's." Slowly she descended the creaking stairs to the street. Maureen said, "Oh, I better go look at the baby. What are you going to do?"

"What is there to do?" He turned and went into the apartment. Everything was the same and not the same. There, the old oilcloth with the worn corners on the kitchen counter, a pattern of cherries falling into bowls. The kerosene heater standing between the windows. Normally it would have been taken down to the bin in the cellar by Memorial Day; then brought back up around Columbus Day. On the wall the red electric clock with the cracked frame. The calendar from Kretchmer's Bakery. The worn linoleum patterned to resemble a Persian rug, the pattern worn away at the stove and the sink. The gas stove and oven with the animal-like legs, the porcelain of the old sink worn away under the dripping faucet. The coffee in the canister; in the 'Flour' canister was the bread to keep it away from the mice that no one had, in the 'Sugar' canister was the sugar still in its bag, in the 'Tea' was the needle and thread, and tape measure and scissors and the collection of buttons. The box of tea bags was in the cupboard. To reach the top shelf his mother had to stand on a chair. The place was really a railroad flat of five rooms with no doors between except for the bathroom. With mom and dad gone from it, it quickly lost any charm it held in his memory of childhood. Mom and dad had slept nearest the kitchen, then Maureen with her orange crate dressing table with a skirt tacked around it, then his 'room', then the front room, which overlooked the street four floors below.

There was no closet in his room. He had a metal locker. He tried on his high school suit jacket. The sleeves were too short and he could no longer button the front. He pondered buying a new suit but could not muster the energy to go downtown. He would stay in his uniform and had his raincoat. He always associated funerals with rain. At his grandfather's a woman strayed off the stepping stone path and got bogged down in the muddy grass. She pulled up her foot without the shoe, which filled with muddy water, balancing on the one foot until a man noticed and rescued her. Maureen and he could not stop laughing. Whenever they talked of grandpa whose memory faded quickly they remembered the woman with the shoe and laughed again. Grandpa had a big white yellow moustache and drove a coal truck, which they never saw. Vincent reached into the bottom of his locker and took out the coffee can of marbles, moonies, staries, and favorite shooters. They were beautiful, the swirling milky whites and reds and blues with clear veins separating them. He dumped them out on the worn spread and ran his hand over them. How long ago it was now that they had claimed all his attention, He might trade one from time to time but not sell a one for all the tea in China.

Maureen came up with the baby. She laid him on the first bed. Vincent stood over him and scratched his belly. He laughed. Maureen set up the old ironing board and began to iron a dress, "This will have to do for today. Tomorrow I'll go down to A&S and pick up something black. I hate black. They probably don't even have anything in maternity in black. I know if I went into one of those little shops I could find something but who can afford those prices?"

He took his wallet out of his sock and put three tens on the table, "Here. I got plenty."

"No, Vinnie, you keep it. I'll use mom's charge plate. You'll need it for going out."

"Take it. I'm not going out anyplace. It's been piling up for ten months. We had a guy in our outfit never drew any pay. Played cards every night. Never lost. I used to go to Battalion with him, to the Post Office to get Money Orders to send his winnings home to his girlfriend. There's a five hundred dollar limit on Money Orders and he always had to get two of them because he'd have more than five hundred. Some times he'd give me money to hold for him for a couple of days. Guys knew he carried a lot of dough. A lot of sore losers said he cheated. But he didn't have to. He was never reckless. He could read guys' faces. He was a real pro."

"So where is he? Is he still there?"

"Ritchie Flanagan, from the Bronx. He's dead. Shot through the neck by a sniper. Right here." he pointed to his collar bone where it comes near the throat, "Maureen, the iron!" He could smell the rayon smoldering.

"Oh, shit! I almost singed it. But anyway thank God you're home safe. So your friend got shot. My God."

197

"He wasn't my friend. Did I say he was my friend? Just a guy in my squad. It doesn't pay to make friends over there."

"Well, anyway, you'll be getting out soon, won't you?"

"In November. Still got three months to go. Maybe they'll keep me at the Navy Yard."

"Are you going to call Bernadette? She said you stopped writing. Every time I'd see her in the stores she'd ask if we heard from you."

"No, that's over."

"What happened?"

"High School shit. Forget it."

Maureen shrugged, "Think you'll go to college or something? You got the G.I. Bill right?"

"Yeah, maybe. I don't know."

"Never too soon to make plans, mama always used to say."

"Plans." Vinnie stood up and went to the window. The pane of glass that had been broken when he went away to Parris Island was still broken, held in place with successive applications of weathered Scotch Tape. "You don't make plans in Korea."

Mister Flood met them at the door and after his condolences sat them down next to his roll topped desk, his office, divided from the first parlor only by a heavy purple drape. There were some papers to sign. Maureen did it.

Mister Flood said, "Of course your father's insurance will pay for his funeral. But now do you know if your mother had a policy?"

Vinnie and Maureen looked at each other.

"Well, when you go home later, look through your parents' papers. See if she had any life insurance." he stood up and smoothed his black vest under his black jacket. "Shall we go in, then?"

198

Vinnie wondered how he would have taken all this if he had not seen people die already, seen them lined up by the side of the road, covered with blankets and ponchos splattered with mud, buff colored cards attached to the button holes of their field jackets or dungaree jackets. Sometimes there was a problem with I.D. and you were asked by a corpsman to take a look. He'd flick back a corner of the blanket. The face, grey white, young, pinched expression with a hint of surprise. No, you didn't know him, you turned away nauseous. Across the road, next to a stock pile of c-rations and ammo, some guys hunkered down drinking coffee out of their canteen cups, whispering, aware for a short while what flies they were waiting to be swatted.

Vinnie trailed behind. They went into the rear parlor first. Maureen went right up to the polished coffin and knelt on the kneeler, blessed herself and said a prayer. Vinnie was so aware of his legs and his socks and his shoes and sweat under his armpits and his heart racing and his throat constricting. He eased up behind Maureen and looked down into the coffin. He was relieved. He did not recognize his mother. She had lost so much weight and the hairstyle. She never wore her hair like that. The only time he remembered his mother ever going to the beauty parlor was for Maureen's wedding. Maureen motioned for him to kneel beside her. He knelt and blessed himself but he couldn't pray. When he first arrived in Korea, one day all the Catholics were ordered to fall down to the Chaplain's jeep, which had just pulled, into the company street. The priest was a jovial guy who resembled the actor Pat O'Brien with a gray crew cut. The guy next to Vinnie poked him, "Hey, <u>Angels with Dirty Faces</u>, eh?" They had to stifle a laugh. The chaplain told them that Thursday would be Sunday in their company. He would try to say mass every Thursday in their company. Pass the word; he knew there were more Catholics in this outfit than had shown up. Vinnie poked his neighbor to direct his attention to a lieutenant standing a ways off. "That prick! I didn't know he was a Catholic." Mass would be said in the mess tent. Sitting on the first bench inside the tent was a large copybook in which you were to sign your name when you came to mass. The first Sunday after Maloney was hit Vinnie took up the book and scribbled his buddy's name on each page for the past several Sundays.

As Vinnie was standing next to his father's coffin Mrs. Doyle came up to him in the black straw hat she wore summer and winter. She linked her arm in his and said, "Flood can make you look dignified, can't he?" And then to the coffin, "Well, Frank, the worst you ever done was steal a few milk bottles for booze. You'll be ahead on line before many a bishop, I can tell you that."

After Vincent's mumbling words back and forth with half the neighborhood, Philly, in his gray sharkskin suit with the tie draped from his breast pocket took Vinnie aside, "Last chance to cut out. I just seen Father Collins coming up the street to say the rosary at the wake. You wanna spend the next hour on your knees or hoist a few with me in Degnan's?"

Degnan's was crowded and smoky. There were several guys from the neighborhood home on leave or pass from Fort Dix so Vinnie didn't stand out in his uniform. Windy Dinellan who leased a stool at the far end of the bar passed them, "Hey, Vinnie, where you been?"

Philly said, "In Korea, Windy. It's been in all the papers."

"Oh, yeah. Hey, they still fighting over there or what?"

Vinnie just stared at Windy.

Windy said to Philly, "What'id I say?"

Mr. Degnan motioned them around the side of the bar and leaned on the counter with his back to the mirror so he could keep an eye on Joey and the bar and still carry on a conversation. They talked of this and that. Vinnie said thanks for the flowers. Philly said did you see the piece Kretchmer's sent? Not from the drivers but from the old man himself? Well, he could afford it the cheap squarehead."

Somebody shouted over, "Hey, Philly. There's going to be another cop's test in September. Maybe third time will be lucky for you."

"A comedian. With your flat feet you should be on the top of the list."

Mr. Degnan said, "You know, Vinnie your father tried to get out of the bakery. Tried to get on the Fire Department. Bill Doyle took him around to see some people. He couldn't make the height. Just a half inch short. But during the Depression you had to be perfect, you know. I called up Packy Reilly, the Alderman, no soap. There were a hundred thousand guys lined up for two thousand jobs."

Vinnie said, "I didn't know that. He never talked about it."

"Well, Frank was never one to cry over spilt milk."

When Philly saw Mister Kretchmer come through the front door, he took a step backwards. August Kretchmer was a tall beer barrel with arms and legs like logs. His neck and hat size were the same. Philly worked for him but reminded himself that Degnan's was his home turf. Still, there was always Monday morning. Mr. Degnan with a deft swipe of his bar rag and a mumbled aside to some regulars created a roomy space at the bar next to Vincent. Mr. Kretchmer and Mr. Degnan knew each other by reputation. They each always took a full page in St. Theresa's annual journal at the bazaar in September.

Philly danced from one foot to the other, "Hello Mr. Kretchmer. Long way from Long Island, eh?"

"Ja, long way."

With a final swipe of the rag Mr. Degnan said, "Yes sir, what can we get you?"

"Ah, Mister Degnan. Full house tonight, very good."

"Ah, just the usual." said Mr. Degnan, smiling to the ring of the cash register.

"A small ginger ale for me and whatever the boys are hafing. And please, you haf one wit us, ja?"

"Coming up."

Philly said, "That was a nice floral piece you sent Mister Kretchmer.", kicking Vinnie.

"Oh yeah. Thank you for the flowers, Mister Kretchmer. My sister and I, we appreciate the thought."

"It's nutting, nutting. Please accept my condolences for your mother and father. A tragedy. There you are in the war and this happens at home. Who can understand it? Not me."

Philly said, "Yeah, who can fathom it all?"

Mr. Kretchmer craned his neck around taking in the crowded bar. "So, Vincent, could we maybe talk for a minute?

"Sure."

"Let's go over here."

Mr. Kretchmer and Vinnie stood under the shelf holding the television set. Philly wishing he was a fly on the wall.

Mr. Kretchmer said, "You know, Vincent, there is something I want to tell you about your father you know or maybe you don't know. But more time I dont want it to pass in case you shouldn't know what kind of a man your father was. Maybe eight nine years ago we had an accident at the bakery. A man slipped into the machinery. He screamed. I turned off the master switch. His arm was caught in the gears, mangled. The blood. We couldn't get to him. We called the ambulance. He was bleeding pretty good and screaming. We all stood around, hopeless. What could we do? To dismantle the machinery would take hours. Now his blood was running near our feet. Your father crawled under the machinery and got to the man. To this day I don't know how he did it. Even the mechanics who service the conveyor, they never would crawl under the equipment. Even though the power was off, there was springs and levers and worm gears that could still turn just a half inch and cut off your finger or your nose. Like a snake he crawled in there. He took off his belt and made a thing, a..."

"A tourniquet?"

"Ja, one of them. He saved the man's life. Even when the ambulance came, they could do nothing until the conveyor was at least partially taken apart. All that time your father was alone in there with the man. At least an hour. Blood everywhere. We said, "Frank, what can we do? Tell us what to do?" He only shrugged and smiled. That smile the Irish haf; resigned but cocky. The ambulance men told him to every once in a while loosen the tourniquet and then tighten it. I told the mechanics you work like hell or you're fired. We thought the man died but he only passed out. That was a good thing the ambulance man said."

All this time, Vinnie just stared at a scuff mark on the bar rail.

"After, I made him take off the uniform and put on a new one. He couldn't go home like that. A reporter for the <u>News</u> came around. Your father wouldn't talk to him. The next day I called him into the office. I wanted to do something for him. I offered him money. He wouldn't take it. Two more weeks vacation on top of his two weeks. No! He couldn't take it. It would be the same as taking money. He said he couldn't take money for that. That's the kind of a man your father was. Maybe he drank too much sometimes. Said stupid things sometimes. But nobody ever laughed at Frank Mannion at the bakery, not ever again."

Mr. Kretchmer surveyed the smoky, noisy bar, "Nobody in here could shine his shoes."

They went back to Flood's. Maureen was holding forth like she'd been doing it all her life, a woman on either side of her each holding a hand of hers and telling her what grand souls Helen and Frank were and what a brave girl she was and was she going to hang onto the apartment or what because one of them had a niece who was getting married.

On the last night of the wake Mrs. Ryan came over and sat next to Vinnie. Every one was tired and talked out. It was like seeing a play for the third time that you didn't like the first time. Mrs. Ryan leaned over and said, "He was a good ball player in high school. We all used to go over to the Parade Grounds to watch them. Run like a deer he could."

Vinnie said, "Yeah, he loved the Dodgers."

Your mother and I would go to parties in people's houses, you know. And after Frank got rid of his shyness, after a couple of beers, he'd get up and sing the latest songs. Sort of like Russ Columbo he sounded. Helen, your mother, I'd have to sit her down she'd go so weak in the knees. She was cute."

204

"He always sang around the house."

"Oh, not the same thing. He used to be in the choir in the Pro Cathedral till it got in the way of his social life if you know what I mean. But I don't want you to think he couldn't overcome the drink when he wanted to. He always worked overtime in November and December, all he could get to put something under the tree on Christmas morning for you and Maureen and Helen. I'd be going down to the Deli with the empties from me and Tim, God rest his soul, and I'd see your father passing Degnan's on the far side of the street. He'd wave to me, 'Annie, there's a magnet pulling me over there but I'm resisting it.' He could always make you laugh."

They had a ten o'clock funeral mass at St. Theresa's and by the time they were all standing around the open graves in Holy Cross Cemetery, it was sweltering. Maureen had found a cheap black maternity dress and a small black straw hat. Her hair hung down limp and dull. Beads of perspiration standing on her fair freckled temples. Father Collins intoned the grave side prayers, his red neck cinched by his white starched collar. He looked like he could do with a shooter himself, thought Vinnie and Philly. They knew they could. Hot coppers. At least the cemetery smelled like Prospect Park. That was better than the sickening flowers in Flood's musty funeral parlor.

Vinnie stayed around for a week. He got up each morning and with chipped coffee cup in hand roamed the apartment searching for his mom and dad; each day the trail got colder and colder until he could no longer remember the words to Toora loora loora or catch a scent of lily-of-the-valley. He reported in early to the Brooklyn Navy Yard. When the lease on the apartment was up Maureen told the super Vinnie

205

wouldn't be back. He never saw the place again but for years later some mornings he'd wake up smelling the garbage cans down in the hall. Months later, on guard duty late at night alone he remembered the marbles he had left behind, the tears flowed, and after awhile he agreed with himself it was just as well that he hadn't had to decide what to with the marbles, excess baggage.

Vinnie learned to distance himself from his father to avoid a display of his contempt. In Korea he did the same thing; convincing himself he didn't care about the people who were killed. Because he could not endure mourning their loss and continue to function, to survive, he defined them as strangers, which is especially convenient if one of them has saved your life. For then there is no one for you to owe. The most self-centered must even fleetingly wonder why they are left to wander the earth while their buddy is snuffed out right next to them.

More truths can slip out at a wake than in a lifetime across the dinner table. He had known nothing of his father's dreams and disappointments. Understanding does not always come like a flash of lightening parting the night but more often like a fog slowly burning off in the midmorning of life. It was a sin, he knew, to hate his father so he had learned to ignore him. Now he must search for him and for a way to give him the love and respect he owed his father. OK, picking up on this was growing up, but the flipside was learning it too late to take his father, warts and all, into Degnan's, and buy him a beer, side with him over the game, maybe firmly guide him home to bed when the night was over.

Previously published In the NY Advocate

Beyond the Wicket Door.   April/May 1996, V.10 No. 2)

C-A-T, Cat. June/July 2007.V..21, No 3.

Fear. Aug/Sept, 1995,V.7, No.4)

The Blue Sweater. Aug/Sept. 1994, V.8,No.4.

The Personal Touch. Aug/Sept. 1998, V.12, No.4.

The   Undertaker's   Apprentice.   Oct./Nov.1999, V.13,. No.5.